Rylee twisted in her seat so that she was facing him.

Her smile was sad and her eyes luminous. He thought of their kiss and wished he could kiss her again.

"Is this a fresh start?" she asked.

"I think so. I'd like it to be."

She reached out and took his hand. He stroked the back of hers with his thumb.

"And you're willing to work with me?" she asked.

"I'll do everything I can to help you."

"Wonderful. One of the groups we are now targeting is the Congregation of Eternal Wisdom. You're familiar?"

Despite the warmth of the room, a chill rolled up Axel's spine and into his chest until his heart iced over. He drew back, leaning against the armrest.

Was he familiar? He was. But he did not want to be the one to bring Rylee to them.

WARNING SHOT

JENNA KERNAN

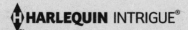

For Jim, always.

ISBN-13: 978-1-335-60472-9

Warning Shot

Copyright © 2019 by Jeannette H. Monaco

Recycling programs
for this product may
not exist in your area.

Printed in U.S.A.

Jenna Kernan has penned over two dozen novels and received two RITA® Award nominations. Jenna is every bit as adventurous as her heroines. Her hobbies include recreational gold prospecting, scuba diving and gem hunting. Jenna grew up in the Catskills and currently lives in the Hudson Valley in New York State with her husband. Follow Jenna on Twitter, @jennakernan, on Facebook or at jennakernan.com.

Books by Jenna Kernan

Harlequin Intrigue

Protectors at Heart

Defensive Action
Adirondack Attack
Warning Shot

Apache Protectors: Wolf Den

Surrogate Escape
Tribal Blood
Undercover Scout
Black Rock Guardian

Apache Protectors: Tribal Thunder

Turquoise Guardian
Eagle Warrior
Firewolf
The Warrior's Way

Apache Protectors

Shadow Wolf
Hunter Moon
Tribal Law
Native Born

Harlequin Historical

Gold Rush Groom
The Texas Ranger's Daughter
Wild West Christmas
A Family for the Rancher
Running Wolf

Harlequin Nocturne

Dream Stalker
Ghost Stalker
Soul Whisperer
Beauty's Beast
The Vampire's Wolf
The Shifter's Choice

Visit the Author Profile page at Harlequin.com.

CAST OF CHARACTERS

Axel Trace—Decorated Army MP turned local sheriff of Onutake County in New York State with a troubling past that he will do anything to keep buried.

Rylee Hockings—Ambitious Department of Homeland Security agent on her first field assignment who aims to make a break in her investigation.

Sorrel Vasta—Acting executive director of the Kowa-Onaharie tribe of the Mohawk nation.

Stanley Coopersmith—Head of a colony of doomsday survivalists living on the New York side of the US–Canadian border.

Hal Mondello—Community leader and moonshiner.

Father Wayne—Leader of a religious order with radical end-of-times beliefs.

Kurt Rogers—Former sheriff and Axel's mentor.

Lloyd Futterman—Head of the motorcycle gang the North Country Riders.

Chapter One

Homeland Security Agent Rylee Hockings paused on the way into the sheriff's office at the foul language booming from the side of the building. The deep baritone voice continued in a colorful string of obscenities that made her think the speaker had been in some branch of the armed services.

A military brat herself, she had heard her fair share of cussing during her formative years while being dragged from one base to another, Kyoto to Hawaii to Germany and back to Hawaii. The youngest of six, she had the distinction of being the only one of her family not to join the US Marines. Some of the military upbringing had worn off on her because she still believed that one was judged on performance. It was one of many reasons she planned to kill this assignment and show her supervisor she had what it took to be a field operative.

It was just past noon on Labor Day. Because of the federal holiday, she had not expected to find the sheriff in his office, but stopped as a courtesy. The second day of September and sunny, but the sunshine did not warm this frozen block of a county in upstate New York. Here it already felt like November. The leaves were pretty. Already at peak leaf-peeping season.

She rounded the building and found a tall man with strands of honey-blond hair falling over his flushed face as he jammed a coat hanger in the slot between the weather stripping and the driver's side window of the vehicle before him.

The vehicle was a white SUV and on the side panel in gold paint was the county seal and the word *Sheriff.*

The man had his back to her and he had not heard her approach due to the swearing and stomping of his feet on the frozen ground. His breath showed in the blast of cold air. The collar of his jacket was turned up against the chill. His distraction gave her a moment to admire an unobstructed view of one of the nicest looking butts she had seen in some time. His uniform slacks were just tight enough and his posterior just muscular enough to keep her interest for a little too long. He wore a brown nylon jacket, heavily padded and flapping at his sides as he threw the coat hanger to the ground.

"Unsat," she said, using the US Marine jargon for unsatisfactory.

He whirled and met her gaze by pinning her with eyes so blue they should have belonged to a husky. Her smile dropped with her stomach. Straight nose, square chin and a sensual mouth, the guy was the complete package, and then he opened his mouth.

"Sneaking up on a sheriff is a bad idea."

"As bad as locking your keys inside?" She squinted her eyes and dragged her sunglasses down her nose. "I could have had an entire unit with me, and you wouldn't have heard."

He stooped to retrieve his twisted coat hanger, snatching it from the ground with long elegant fingers.

"FUBAR," she said.

"You in the Corps?" he asked, referring to the US Marine Corps.

"My father, two brothers and a sister." She motioned to the sheriff's vehicle. "No spare?"

"Lost them," he admitted.

"Why not use a Slim Jim?"

He scowled and thumbed over his shoulder. "It's in the back."

She wished she'd checked into the background of the sheriff of Onutake County before this meeting, but time had been limited. Knowing what he looked like would have been helpful right about now. For all she knew, this guy was a car thief.

She made a note to do some background checking as soon as she found a moment.

"You Sheriff Trace?"

"Who's asking?"

"Rylee Hockings, Department of Homeland Security." She retrieved her business card case from her blazer and offered him a card, leaning forward instead of stepping closer. There was something other than his vocabulary that urged her to keep her distance. She listened to that voice instead of the one that wondered if he were single. But her traitorous eyes dropped to his bare hands and the left one, which held no wedding band.

He nodded, not looking at her card.

"Didn't expect to find you on the job today, Sheriff."

"More calls on weekends and holidays. Just the way of the world."

He'd have trouble responding without his car, she thought.

"What can I do you for?"

"Just an introduction. Courtesy visit."

"Uh-huh," he said, his expression turning skeptical. "So, you plan on treating me like I'm still a marine?"

"Excuse me?"

"Muscles are required, intelligence not essential," he said, choosing one of the tired jokes members of the army often leveled at the marines.

"So you were army, then." She knew that much from the jibe toward her family's branch of the military.

"Once." He smiled and her heart jumped as if hit with a jolt of electricity. The smile and those eyes and jaw and, holy smokes, she was in trouble. She forced a scowl.

"You know, you should always run a check of your equipment before you lock up."

"You a newbie, reading manuals, going by the book?"

She was and the assumption was insulting.

"Why do you ask?"

"You still have that new car smell."

Her scowl was no longer forced. What did that even mean? "I'm not the one locked out of my unit."

"It isn't even locked. The alarm is just on and I didn't want to set it off again."

Again. How often did he do this? she wondered. "I'll be doing some investigating in your county."

"What kind of investigating?"

She smiled. "Nice to meet you, Sheriff."

"You want an escort?"

"From a sheriff careless enough to leave his keys and—" she glanced through the windshield to verify her suspicion "—his phone in his unit? Thank you but I'll manage."

She turned to go. *New car smell*. She growled and marched away.

"You got a Slim Jim in your vehicle, Hockings?" he called after her.

"I do, but I wouldn't want to chance damaging yours. Maybe try Triple A."

"Where you headed?"

"Kowa Nation," she said and then wished she hadn't.

"Hey!"

Rylee turned back. Throwing her arms out in exasperation. "What?"

"They know you're coming?"

"Where's the fun in that?"

"Agent Hockings, I advise you to call the tribal leadership and make a formal request to visit."

She cast him the kind of wave that she knew was dismissive. Those damn blue eyes narrowed. They were still enthralling. As blue as the waters of the Caribbean.

Rylee straightened her shoulders and kept going. When she reached the front of the building, she heard the sheriff's car alarm blare and then cut short.

From her official vehicle, Rylee logged in to the laptop affixed to the dash and checked out the sheriff's official records. Sheriff Axel Trace had been taken into state custody at thirteen and listed as orphaned. She gazed at the entry. There was a hole there big enough to drive a truck through. No birth record or school records. His paper trail, as they used to call it, began with the entry by the sheriff of this very county when he took custody of the lad. Axel's parents were listed as deceased, but no names for her to search. No cause of their deaths or circumstances, no guardians noted, no relatives. Just record of Axel's temporary placement with Kurt Rogers, the county sheriff at the time. The placement lasted five years until Axel enlisted out of high school. Rylee scanned and clicked and scanned some more. Impressed didn't quite cover it. There were plenty of records now, and all exemplary. She'd read them more carefully later. But on a fast pass, the man had distinguished himself in the US Army as an MP and reaching the rank of captain in Iraq. She scanned his records and noted his transfer to Hanau, Germany.

"Oh, no," she said.

Captain Axel Trace had broken up a brawl in a bar that had resulted in the death of two servicemen. She would read all the details later. For now, she skimmed and noted that Trace had been attacked and engaged with appropriate use of force.

"And two months later, you chose discharge rather than reenlistment." She wondered if the incident had been the cause of his decision to leave the service and his prospects behind.

He seemed to have had a great opportunity for advancement and she wondered why he had instead elected discharge and returned to his home county to run for sheriff, replacing the man who had held the position until retirement six years ago. It seemed an odd choice.

Perhaps it was just her ambition talking, but the sheriff could have done a lot better than this frozen Klondike Bar of a county. The entire northern border was Canada and, other than the St. Lawrence River, she saw nothing but trees and more trees. She didn't understand why anyone with his training would allow himself to get stuck in a crappy, freezing county where you reached the highest possible position at thirty. Sheriff Trace had no family up here, none anywhere according to his records. And now he had nowhere to go but sideways and no increase in salary unless the good people of the county wanted their taxes raised.

Meanwhile, Rylee had nothing but advancement in her sights. Her plans included filling in that blank spot in her résumé under field experience. Eliminating the possible terrorist threats up here was a good start. She wasn't fooled that this was a great opportunity. This county had been tagged by the DHS analysts as the least likely spot for the crossing. But that didn't make it impossible. This morning she had gotten her break. Her initial assignment was to speak to four groups who might be connected with the terrorist organization calling itself Siming's Army. Just initial interviews, but it was a start. But en route, Border Patrol called her to report an illegal crossing: a single male who was carrying a canvas duffel bag. The contents of that bag were her objective. Until she knew otherwise, she'd act as if the contents of the bag was the object for which her entire department hunted. They had abandoned pursuit when the target entered onto Mohawk land. She had a chance now, a possible break in the search for the entry point of this threat.

Her attempt to reach her boss, Catherine Ohr, ended in a voice mail message, and she had yet to hear back.

She had lost the GPS signal with her directions to the Kowa Mohawk Nation just outside of town. Not that it mattered. One of the things her father had taught her was how to read a map.

Federal officers investigating leads did not need appointments to visit federal land. Sheriff Axel Trace should have known that, but it wasn't her job to tell him what he should know.

Newbie. New car smell. First field assignment.

Rylee lowered her chin and stepped on the gas.

Chapter Two

Sheriff Trace responded to the call from the Kowa Nation one hour later, passing the border patrol checkpoint just off their rez and knowing that would only further ruffle feathers. Likely, this was also the work of Rylee Hockings.

Homeland Security Agent Hockings didn't look like trouble, as she sat small and sullen in the seat beside the desk of the Kowa Mohawk Reservation's acting chief of police. But having already met her, he could not help but take in the moment. Having ignored his advice and dismissed him like the help, there was a certain satisfaction in seeing her in wrist restraints.

He didn't know the exact point when his moment to gloat changed into a completely different kind of study, but he now noticed that Rylee Hockings had a heart-shaped face, lips the color of the flesh of a ripe watermelon and large, expressive brown eyes with elegant arching brows that were the brown of dry pine needles. Her straight, fine blond hair fell forward, making her flushed cheeks seem even pinker. Their eyes met, and her brow descended. Her lids cinched as she squinted at him with open hostility.

Axel could not resist smiling. "The next time I ask you if you'd like an escort, maybe don't flip me the bird."

"I didn't flip you off." Her reply was a bark, like a dog that might be either frightened or angry but either way sent clear signs for him to back off.

"No, I believe you said that when you wanted the help of a sheriff who was dumb enough to lock his keys in his cruiser, you'd ask for it."

He glanced at her wrists, secured with a wide plastic zip tie and hammering up and down on the knees of her navy slacks as if sending him a message in Morse code. He wondered why federal agents always advertised their profession with the same outfits. A blazer, dress shirt and slacks with a practical heel was just not what folks wore up here.

"I didn't say dumb enough. I said *careless enough*."

He glanced to the acting chief of police, Sorrel Vasta, who said, "Potato, Pa-tot-o."

"I also mentioned that the Kowa tribe does not do drop-in visits," said Axel.

"Especially from feds," added Vasta. He folded his arms across his chest, which just showed off how very thin and young he really was.

"This," said Agent Hockings, "is federal land. As a federal officer, I do not need permission—"

"You are a trespasser on the Mohawk Nation. We are within our rights to—"

Whatever rights Vasta might have been about to delineate were cut short by the blast of a shotgun.

Hockings threw herself from the chair to the floor

as Vasta ducked behind the metal desk. Axel dropped, landing beside Hockings, pressed shoulder to shoulder.

"Shots fired," she called, reaching for her empty holster with her joined hands and then swearing under her breath.

"Who are you yelling to exactly?" Axel asked. "We all heard it."

She pressed those pink lips together and scowled, then she scrambled along the floor, undulating in a way that made his hairs stand up and electricity shiver over his skin. He hadn't felt that drumbeat of sexual awareness since that day in high school when Tonya Sawyer wore a turquoise lace bra under a T-shirt that was as transparent as a bridal veil. She'd been sent home, of course, to change, but it hadn't mattered. Images like that stuck in the memory like a bug on a fly strip. He had a feeling that the sight of Hockings's rippling across the floor like a wave was going to stick just like that turquoise bra.

"Out of the way," Hockings said, her thigh brushing his shoulder.

The electricity now scrambled his brain as the current shot up and then down to finally settle, like a buzzing transformer, in his groin. High school all over again.

Vasta squatted at the window and peeked out. The only thing he held was the venetian blinds. His gun remained on his hip. He glanced back at Axel and cocked his head.

Axel realized his own mouth was hanging open as if Agent Hockings had slapped him, which she would have, if she knew what he had been thinking.

"They shot her car. Peppered the side," said Vasta.

Her head popped up like a carnival target from be-hind the desk.

"Who did?" Her perfect blond hair was now mussed. Axel resisted the urge to lay the strands back in order. Was her hair silky or soft like angora?

"I dunno, but they are long gone," said Vasta. "Even took the shell."

"How do you know that?" She reached his side.

"Shells are green and red, mostly. Easy to spot on the snow."

Agent Hockings moved to the opposite side of the window. "There is a whole group of people out there. Witnesses."

Axel's laugh gleaned another scowl from Hockings. Vasta's mouth quirked but then fell back to reveal no hint of humor when Hockings turned from Axel to him.

Now Axel was scowling. Vasta was making him look bad, or perhaps he was doing that all on his own.

Axel reached the pair who now stood flanking the window like bookends. He pressed his arm to hers, muscling her out of the way in order to get a glimpse outside. Her athletic frame brought her head to his shoulder, and he was only five foot ten. She was what Mrs. Shubert, the librarian of the Kinsley Public Library, would have called petite. Mrs. Shubert had also been petite and was as mighty as a superhero in Axel's mind. He knew not to judge ferocity in inches.

"Or," said Hockings, "you could see if any of the spectators have a shotgun in their hand or shell casing in their pocket."

"Illegal search," said Vasta. "And none of them have a shotgun any longer. So, here's what's going to happen.

Sheriff Trace is going to escort you out in restraints and put you in the back of his unit. Then he's going to drive you outta here. If you are smart, you will keep your head down and look ashamed, because you should be."

"I will not."

"Then they will likely break every window in Axel's cruiser and possibly turn it over with you both inside."

Hockings stiffened as her eyes went wide with shock. The brown of her irises, he now saw, were flecked with copper. She looked to him, as if asking if Vasta were pulling her leg.

He hoped his expression said that the acting chief of police was not.

She turned back to Vasta. "You'd have to stop them."

"Listen, Agent Hockings, it's just me here. Last week, I was an officer, and now this." He motioned to his chief's badge. "Besides, I'm tempted to help them."

Hockings looked from Vasta to Trace and then back to Vasta.

"Are you pressing charges against Hockings?" Axel asked Vasta.

"Are you serious?" she asked the sheriff.

He gave her a look he hoped said that he was very serious. "They have tribal courts and you do *not* want to go there."

"They can't prosecute a federal agent."

"But can hold you until your people find out."

Her fingers went straight, flexing and then lacing together to create a weapon that he believed she was wise enough not to use.

"Fine. So contrite. That will get us out of here?"

The acting chief of police nodded.

"What about my vehicle?"

"I'll drive it to the border and leave it for you."

"The border?" To Rylee, the border was Canada. Vasta enlightened her.

"The border of our reservation."

Her gaze flicked between them and her full mouth went thin and miserly. But she thought about it. Axel just loved the way the tips of her nose and ears went pink as a rabbit's in her silent fury.

"Fine. Let's get going, if you have your keys," she said, pushing past him.

The acting chief of police was faster, beating them to the door to the main squad room. There, two officers sat on a desk and table respectively, both kicking their legs from their perches where they had been watching the drama playing out through the glass door of the chief's office.

"Josh and Noah, you two have point," said Vasta, instructing the men to lead the escort.

Both men rose, grinning. Each wore tight-fitting uniforms. Josh's hair was black and bristly short. Noah wore his brown hair in a knot at his neck.

They headed out behind the officers, with Axel holding Hockings's taut arm as if she were his prisoner. Behind them came the acting chief of police. Trace tried and failed not to notice that he could nearly encircle Rylee's bicep with his thumb and index finger and that included her wool coat. She glared up at him and her muscle bunched beneath his grip. Hockings clearly did not like role-play.

The crowd that Hockings had insisted Vasta question were now calling rude suggestions and booing.

Vasta waved and spoke to them in Kowa, a form of the Iroquoian language. The officers before them peeled away, giving Axel a view of his cruiser and the rear door. For reasons he did not completely understand, his squad car was untouched. Axel hit the fob, unlocking his unit. Noah swept the rear door open.

Axel made a show of putting his hand on Hockings's head to see that she was safely ensconced in the rear of his unit. The effect brought a cheer from the peanut gallery and allowed him to get the answer to one of his many questions about Hockings.

Her hair was soft as the ear of an Irish setter and blond right to the roots. Hockings fell to her side across the rear seat and remained on her side. *Wise beyond her years*, he thought.

The booing resumed as he climbed behind the wheel. It pleased him that Josh and Noah now stood between his unit and the gathering of pissed-off Mohawks.

And off they went. They were outside of Salmon River, the tribe's main settlement, but still on rez land before Rylee sat up and laced her fingers through the mesh guard that separated his front from the back seat. Her fingernails were shiny with clearish pink polish and neatly filed into appealing ovals. Her wrists were no longer secured.

"How did you get out of that?" he asked.

"My father says you can measure a person's IQ by whether or not they carry a pocketknife."

"With the exception being at airports?" he asked.

"You going to keep me back here the entire way?"

"Not if you want to sit beside me."

She didn't answer that, just threw herself back into

the upholstery and growled. Then she looked out the side window.

"They better not damage my car," she muttered.

"More," he said.

"What?"

She wasn't looking at him. He knew because he was staring at her in the rearview until the grooves in the shoulder's pavement vibrated his attention back to the road.

"Damage your car more," he clarified. "They already shot at it. So, you find who you were looking for?"

She folded her arms over her chest. Just below her lovely small breasts, angry fists balled. She was throwing so much shade the cab went dark.

"How do you know I was looking for someone?"

"What Home Security does, isn't it, here on the border?"

"In this case, yes. We have an illegal crossing and the suspect fled onto Kowa lands."

"They have your suspect?"

"Denied any knowledge."

Homeland Security Agent Rylee Hockings was about as welcome in Salmon River as a spring snowstorm.

"Maybe Border Patrol has your guy."

"No. They lost 'em. That's why they called me. They abandoned pursuit when our suspect crossed onto Mohawk land. Both the suspect and the cargo have vanished." She glanced back the way they had come. "I need my car."

What she needed were social skills. She didn't want his help, but she might need it. And he needed to get her out of his county before she got into something way more dangerous than ruffled Mohawk regalia. Up here on the border, waving a badge at the wrong people could get you killed.

The woman might have federal authority and a mission, but she didn't know his county or the people here. Folks who lived on the border did it for one of three reasons. Either it was as far away from whatever trouble they had left as they could get, or they had business on the other side. He'd survived up here by knowing the difference, doing his job and not poking his nose into the issues that were not under his purview.

There was one other reason to be up here. If you had no other choice. Rylee had a choice. So she needed to go. Sooner was better.

He considered himself to be both brave and smart, but that would be little to no protection from Rylee's alluring brown eyes and watermelon-pink mouth. Best way he knew to keep clear of her was to get her south as soon as possible.

"The Mohawk are required to report illegal entry onto US soil," she said. "And detain if possible. They did neither."

"Maybe they aren't interested in our business or our borders."

"America's business? Is that what you mean?"

He scratched the side of his head and realized he needed a haircut. "It's just my experience that the Mohawk people consider themselves separate from the United States and Canada." He half turned to look back at her. "You know they have territory in both countries."

"Yes, I was briefed. And smuggling, human trafficking and dope running happen in your county."

She'd left out moonshining. But border security was thankfully not his job. Neither were the vices that were handled by ATF—the federal agency responsible for alcohol, tobacco, firearms and recently explosives. He was glad because enforcement was a dangerous, impossible and thankless assignment. His responsibilities, answering calls from citizens via EMS, traffic stops and accidents made up the bulk of his duties. He was occasionally involved with federal authorities, collaborating only when asked, and Agent Hockings seemed thrilled to do everything herself. He should leave it at that.

"Borders bring their own unique troubles."

"Yet, you have made limited arrests related to these activities. Mostly minor ones, at that, despite the uptick in illegal activities, especially in winter when the river freezes."

He ignored the jibe. He did his duty and that was enough to let him sleep most nights.

"It doesn't always freeze," he said.

"Hmm? What doesn't?"

"The river. Some years it doesn't freeze."

She cocked her head and gave him a look as if he puzzled her. "How long have you been sheriff?"

If she were any kind of an agent, she knew that already, but he answered anyway.

"Going on six years this January."

"You seem young."

"Old enough to know better and halfway to collecting social security."

"You grew up here, didn't you?"

"I've never lived anywhere else."

"You have family up here?"

His smile faltered, and he swerved to the shoulder. He gripped the wheel with more force than necessary and glanced back at her, his teeth snapping together with a click.

One thing he was not doing was speaking about his past. Not his time in the military, not the men he'd killed or the ones he couldn't save. And he wasn't ever speaking of the time before the sheriff got him clear of the compound. He needed to get this question machine out of his county, so he could go back to being the well-respected public servant again.

As far as he knew, only two men knew where he came from—his father and the former sheriff. And he looked nothing like that scrawny kid Sheriff Rogers had saved. So changed, in fact, he believed his own father would not know him. At least that was what he prayed for, every damn day. All he wanted in this world was to live in a place where the rules made sense, where he had some control. And where, maybe someday, he and a nice, normal woman could create a family that didn't make his stomach knot. But for now, he needed to be here, watching his father. Here to stop him if he switched from preaching his unhinged religious vision to creating it.

She opened her copper-flecked brown eyes even wider, feigning a look of innocence.

"What?" she asked.

He unlocked his teeth, grinding them, and then pivoted in his seat to stare back at her.

"Two hours ago, you showed up in the city of Kinsley at city hall, making it very clear that you did not want the assistance of the county sheriff. Now you want my résumé."

"Local law enforcement is obliged to assist in federal investigations."

"Which I will do. But you asked about my family. Like to fill in some blanks, that right? Something before I turned thirteen?" She was digging for the details that were not in public records or, perhaps, just filling time. Either way, he was not acting as the ant under her magnifying glass.

She met his stare and did not flinch or look away from the venom that must have been clear in his expression. Instead, she shrugged. "What I want is out of this back seat."

He threw open his door and then yanked open hers. She stared up at him with a contrite expression that did not match the gleam of victory shimmering in the dark waters of her eyes. *Dangerous waters*, he thought. Even through his annoyance, he could not completely squelch the visceral ache caused by her proximity.

"You prefer to drive?" he said.

She slipped out of his vehicle to stand on the road before him. "Not this time. When do I get my vehicle back?"

He drew out his phone and sent a text. By the time she had settled into the passenger side, adjusted both the seat and safety belt, he received a reply.

"It's there now," he said. The photo appeared a moment later and he plastered his hand across his mouth to keep her from seeing his grin. Axel slipped behind the wheel and performed an illegal turn on a double solid, a privilege of his position, and took them back the way they had come.

"Why are you whistling?" she asked.

Was he? Perhaps. It was just that such moments of glee were hard to contain. By the time they reached the sign indicating the border of the Mohawk rez, she caught sight of her vehicle.

Someone had poured red paint over the roof and it was dripping down over both the windows and doors on one side. There were handprints all over the front side panel.

"My car!" she cried, leaning forward for a good look. Then she pointed. "That's damaging federal property."

"Looks like a war horse," he said, admiring the paint job. It was so rare that people got exactly what they deserved.

Chapter Three

Rylee Hockings stood beside the surly sheriff with hands on hips as she regarded the gooey paint oozing from the metallic door panel of her official vehicle and onto the road. She struggled to keep her chin up. Her first field assignment had headed south the minute she headed north. When her boss, Lieutenant Catherine Ohr, saw this car, she would be livid.

Her vehicle had been towed and left just outside the reservation land and abandoned beneath the sign welcoming visitors to the Kowa Nation.

"Maybe the paint will fill in the bullet holes," offered Sheriff Trace.

His chuckle vibrated through her like a call issued into an empty cave. Something about the tenor and pitch made her stomach do a funny little tremble. She rested a hand flat against her abdomen to discourage her body from getting ideas.

"I could use those prints as evidence," she said to Sheriff Trace.

"Or you could accept the life lesson that you might be the big cheese where you come from but to the Kowa, you are an outsider. Up here, your position will get you more trouble than respect. Which is why I offered you an escort."

And she had turned him down flat. Despite his mirthful blue eyes, extremely handsome face, brown hair bleached blond from what she presumed was the summer sun, and a body that was in exceptionally good shape, something about this man rubbed her the wrong way. The sheriff seemed to think the entire county belonged to him personally.

"I need to call Border Patrol." She left him to gloat and made her call. Border Patrol had lost their suspects after they entered Mohawk territory yesterday, Sunday, at three in the afternoon and had had no further sightings. Now she understood why they ceased pursuit at their border of the reservation and called her field office. They had set up a perimeter, so the suspect was either still on Mohawk land or had slipped off and into the general population. The chances that this man was *her* man were slim, but until she had word that the package and courier had been apprehended elsewhere, she would treat each illegal border crossing as if the carrier came from Siming's Army.

Her conversation and update yielded nothing further. The perimeter remained in place. All vehicles entering or leaving the American side of the Kowa lands were being checked. They had not found their man.

She stowed her phone and returned the few steps to find her escort watching the clouds as if he had not a thing to do.

"They tell you they wouldn't go on Mohawk land?" he asked.

She didn't answer his question, for he seemed to already know their reply. "So, anyone who wants to avoid apprehension from federal authorities just has to make it onto Mohawk land as if they had reached some home-free base, like in tag."

"No, they have to reach Mohawk's sovereign land and the Mohawk have to be willing to allow them to stay. The Kowa people have rights granted to them under treaties signed by our government."

They had reached another impasse. Silence stretched, and she noticed that his eyes were really a stunning blue-gray.

"You want me to hang around?" he asked, his body language signaling his wish to leave.

"Escort me to a place that can get this paint off," she said.

He touched the paint and then rubbed it between thumb and forefinger. He wiped his finger and thumb on the hood, then tapped his finger up and down to add his fingerprints to the others.

"Stop that!"

He did, holding up his paint-stained hand in surrender. "Oil based. Can't use the car wash. Body shop, I suppose."

"You have one?"

"Not personally, but there is one in town."

"I'll follow." She used her fob to open the door and nothing happened.

He lowered his chin and lifted his brows. The corners of his mouth lifted before he twisted his lips in a poorly veiled attempt to hide his smile.

Had the vandals disconnected her battery or helped themselves to the entire thing?

"Tow truck," he said.

She faced the reservation sign, lifted a stone from the road and threw it. The rock made a satisfying *thwack* against the metal surface.

He placed the call and she checked in with her office. No messages.

"Tow truck will be here in twenty minutes. Want to wait or grab a ride with me?"

"What do I do with the keys?"

"Tow truck doesn't need those," he said.

She nodded. "I knew that."

Did she sound as green as she felt? How much more experience in the field did Trace have? He'd been an army MP and now was a sheriff.

"How did you decide to run for sheriff?" she asked.

His mouth tipped downward. He didn't seem fond of speaking about his past. She decided to find out why that was. She'd missed something in her hasty check.

"My friend and mentor, Kurt Rogers, was retiring. He held on until I got out of the service and threw his support behind me. Been reelected once since then."

Rylee managed to retrieve her briefcase and suitcase from the trunk, half surprised to see them there and not covered with paint. They walked back to his sheriff's unit side by side.

"Must be hard to be popular in this sort of work."

He cocked his head. "I don't find it so."

He helped her place her luggage in the rear seat and then held the passenger door for her. She had her belt clipped as they pulled back on the highway.

They did not speak on the ride into town. The air

in the cruiser seemed to hold an invisible charge. She shifted uncomfortably in her seat and he rubbed his neck.

"Motel or the body shop?" he asked as they hit the limits of the town of Kinsley, which was the county seat.

"Motel."

It bothered her that, of the three possible choices, he took her directly to the place where she was staying. She didn't ask how he knew.

The sheriff pulled to a stop and she retrieved her bags.

He stood on his side of the vehicle, staring across the roof at her. "You feel like telling me where you'll be next, or should I just follow the sound of gunfire?"

She refused to take the bait and only thanked him for the lift.

"Don't mention it," he said and then added, as he slipped back into his unit, "I surely wouldn't."

She stooped to glare at him through the open passenger door. "Why not?"

"You won't need to. Soon everyone in the county will know you are here and what happened on Mohawk land, because a good story spreads faster than wildfire and because you used exactly the sort of strong-arm tactics I'd expect from a rookie agent. What I can't figure is why your supervisor sent you up here without a babysitter. You that unpopular he couldn't even find you a partner? Or is he just that stupid?"

"*She* is not stupid and it's an honor to be given a solo assignment," she said, feeling her face heat. "A show of respect."

"Is that what she told you?"

She slammed the door and he laughed. Rylee stood, fuming, as he cruised out of the lot.

What did she care what he thought? She had work to do. Important work. And she didn't need the approval of the sheriff of one of the most sparsely populated counties in the state.

Kowa Mohawk people were on her watch list along with a motorcycle gang calling themselves the North Country Riders. This gang was known to smuggle marijuana across the Canadian border. Additionally, she needed to investigate a family of moonshiners. The Mondellos had for years avoided federal tax on their product by making and distributing liquor. Finally, and most troubling of all, was a survivalist compound headed by Stanley Coopersmith. Their doomsday predictions and arsenal of unknown weapons made them dangerous.

This was Rylee's first real field assignment and they had sent her solo, which was an honor, no matter what the sheriff said. She was unhappy to be given such an out-of-the-way placement because all the analysis indicated this as the least likely spot for Siming's Army to use for smuggling. Most of department had moved to the Buffalo and Niagara Falls regions where the analysis believed Siming's Army would attempt infiltration.

She let herself into her room and went to work on her laptop. She took a break at midafternoon to head out to the mini-mart across the street to buy some drinks and snacks.

Her car arrived from the body shop just after six o'clock, the telltale outline of the red paint still visible along with the outline of three handprints.

"Couldn't get those out without buffing. Best we could do," said the gaunt tow truck driver in navy blue coveralls. "Also replaced the battery."

"Dead?" she asked.

"Gone," he said.

He clutched a smoldering half-finished cigarette at his side and her invoice in the other. The edges of the brown clipboard upon which her paperwork sat were worn, rounded with age.

She offered her credit card. He copied the numbers and she signed the slip.

The tow truck operator cocked his head to study the vehicle's new look with watery eyes gone yellow with jaundice. "Almost looks intentional. Like those cave paintings in France. You know?"

Rylee flicked her gaze to the handprints and then back to the driver.

"Like a warrior car. I might try something like it with an airbrush."

Rylee her held out her hand for the receipt.

"If I were you, I'd stay off Mohawk land. Maybe stick to the casino from now on."

She accepted the paperwork without comment. The driver folded the pages and handed them to her. Rylee returned to her room and her laptop. It was too late to head out to the next group on her watch list. That would have to wait until tomorrow.

Her phone chimed, alerting her to an incoming call. The screen display read *Catherine Ohr*, and she groaned. She couldn't know about the car already.

"Did you not understand the Mohawk are a sovereign nation?" said her boss.

"On federal land."

"On Kowa Mohawk Nation land. When I asked you to speak to them, I meant you should make an appointment."

"At eight a.m., Border Patrol notified me of a runner. A single male who crossed the border on foot carrying a large navy blue duffel bag. He was believed to have been dropped off by his courier on the Canadian side. That same courier then picked him up on the US side. They were sighted on River Road. Border Patrol detained the pickup driver thirty minutes later just outside Mohawk lands. The passenger fled on foot onto the reservation, carrying the large duffel on his back."

"They questioned the driver?"

"Yes. He denies picking anyone up."

"Name?"

"Quinton Mondello. Oldest son of Hal Mondello."

"How many sons does he have?"

"Four. Quinton runs things with his father. He's the heir apparent, in my opinion."

"So, the moonshiners were carrying moonshine. Made a drop in Canada and were heading home with an empty truck."

"Then why run?"

"You believe the passenger was an illegal immigrant?"

"At the very least," said Rylee.

"You believe the Mondello family is engaged in human trafficking?"

"Or they are assisting the Siming terrorist."

"That's a stretch. Border Patrol saw the passenger flee?"

Rylee's stomach knotted. "No. They were acting

on an anonymous tip who reported seeing the passenger flee prior to Border Patrol's arrival. Border Patrol stopped a truck of similar description just outside Mohawk lands."

"Could have been a Mohawk carrying cigarettes from Canada. Could have been a moonshiner. Pot grower. Poacher. And their tip could have been a rival poacher, moonshiner or pot grower. Any of those individuals would have reason to flee. Hell, they have ginseng hunters up here trespassing all the time."

"Not in the fall."

Ohr made a sound like a growl that did not bode well for Rylee's career advancement plans.

"It could also be a suspect," added Rylee, pushing her luck.

"Therefore, we don't really know if there even was a passenger."

"Quinton Mondello denies carrying a passenger."

"Of course, he does. And he may be telling the truth."

Rylee didn't believe that for a minute.

"So, you decided to follow, alone, without backup and without notifying the tribal police," said Ohr.

Rylee dropped her gaze to the neatly made bed and swallowed, knowing that speaking now would reveal an unwanted tremor in her voice.

"Hockings?"

"Border Patrol didn't pursue." There was that darn tremor.

"Because they understand the law. That is also why they had to release Quinton Mondello. No evidence of wrongdoing."

Silence stretched.

"Do I need to pull you?"

"No, ma'am."

"I do not have time to clean up your messes, Hockings."

Rylee thought of the handprints on her federal vehicle and her head hung in shame.

"Do not go on Mohawk land again for any reason."

"Yes, ma'am."

Ohr hung up on her.

Rylee needed some air. She gathered her personal weapon, wallet, shield and keys before heading out. The September night had turned cooler than she realized, and she ducked inside to grab a lined jacket. She stepped outside again and glanced about. The night had fallen like a curtain, so much blacker than her suburban neighborhood with the streetlights lining every road. Here, only the parking lot and the mini-mart across the road glowed against the consuming dark. She'd seen an ice-cream place, the kind that had a grill, on their arrival. A burger and fries with a shake would hit the spot. It wasn't until she was driving toward her destination that she realized she had snatched the blue windbreaker that had bold white letters across the back, announcing that she was Homeland Security.

The dash clock told her it was nearly 8:00 p.m. and she wondered how long the ice-cream joint might stay open. The answer turned out to be eight o'clock. She arrived to see the lot empty except for one familiar sheriff's vehicle and a clear view of the solitary worker inside, cleaning the grill. Out front, sitting on the picnic table surface with his feet on the bench, was Sheriff Trace and a very young man.

She ignored them, which wasn't easy, as she had to walk from her vehicle to the order window.

"Ms. Hockings," said the sheriff.

She nodded and glanced at the pair.

"Who's that?" asked the young man. The sheriff's companion had peach fuzz on his jaw and hair shaved so short that it was impossible to know if his hair was blond or light brown and a stunned expression. There was an old crescent scar on his scalp where the hair did not grow.

The sheriff mumbled something as she reached the order window and was greeted by a red-faced woman who said, "Just cleaned the grill. You want something to eat, have to be the fryer."

"All right. So…what are my choices?"

"Fried shrimp, mozzarella sticks or French fries."

"Ice cream?"

"Yup." She motioned a damp rag at the menu board behind her. "Ain't cleaned that yet."

Rylee ordered the shrimp and fries with a vanilla shake. The woman had the order up in less than four minutes and the counter light flicked off as Rylee retreated with her dinner in a box lined with a red-and-white-checked paper already turning transparent in the grease.

The sheriff called to her before she could reach her car.

"Agent Hockings. Join us?" he asked.

She let her shoulders deflate. Rylee wanted only to eat and have a shower. But she forced a smile. Establishing working relationships with local law enforcement was part of the job. Unfortunately, this local made her skin tingle when she got too close. She hated knowing from the heat of her face that she was blushing. He returned her smile and her mind wandered to questions that were none of her business, like what Axel Trace's chest looked like beneath that uniform.

Two months ago, Rylee had had a steady boyfriend but that ended when she got promoted and he didn't. The help she'd given him on course work might have worked against him in the written testing when he didn't know the information required. In any case, he blamed her, and she'd broken things off. Showing his true colors made getting over him easy. Except at night. She missed the feel of him in her bed; that had been the only place they had gotten along just fine. Now she knew that attraction was not enough of a foundation for a relationship. So why was she staring at the sheriff's jawline and admiring the gap between his throat and the white undershirt that edged his uniform?

Because, Rylee, you haven't been with a man in a long time. She swept him with a gaze and dismissed this attraction as the second worst idea of the day. The first being pursuit onto Mohawk land.

Rylee sat across from the pair, who slipped from the surface of the picnic table and onto the opposite bench, staring at her in silence as she ate the curling brown breading that must have had a shrimp in there somewhere. The second bite told her the shellfish was still frozen in the center. She pushed it aside.

"Want my second burger?" asked Axel.

"You have a spare?"

"Bought it for Morris, here. But two ought to do him."

Morris gave the burger in the sheriff's hands a look

of regret before dipping the last of his fries into his ice-cream sundae.

"This is Morris Coopersmith," said Trace. "Morris, this is Rylee Hockings. She's with Homeland Security."

Stanley Coopersmith was one of the persons of interest.

Morris's brows lifted, and his hand stilled. When he spoke, his voice broke. "Nice to meet you."

"Likewise." Rylee accepted the wrapped burger Sheriff Trace extended. "Any relationship to Stanley Coopersmith?"

Morris grinned and nodded. "That's my dad." Then the smile waned. "He doesn't like comics."

Morris's dad was on her watch list. He led a colony of like-minded doomsday survivalists, who had their camp right on the New York side of the border. It would be simple for such a group to transport anything or anyone they liked through the woods and over the border in either direction.

"Want some pickles?" asked Morris, offering the ones he had plucked from his burgers.

"No, thank you," she said to Morris. Her phone chimed and she checked to see the incoming text was unimportant.

Morris pointed. "Do you have a camera on that?"

Rylee nodded.

"Take our picture," he insisted and moved closer to the sheriff.

Rylee gave the sheriff a questioning look and received a shrug in response, so she opened the camera app and took a photo.

Morris reached for her phone and she allowed him

to take it and watched closely as he admired the shot. At last, he handed her back her phone.

She asked the sheriff, "Are you two related?"

It was a blind guess. Morris was pink and lanky; his body type more like a basketball player. Axel's blond hair, sun-kissed skin and muscular physique seemed nearly opposite to the boy's.

She wasn't sure why she didn't delete the photo, but she left it and tucked her phone away. Then she turned her attention to her meal. She had a mouthful of burger when the sheriff dispelled her first guess.

"I'm transporting Morris from his home to the jail in Kinsley due to failure to report to his last hearing. He's got to be in court in the morning."

"Oh," she said, forcing the word past the mouthful of food. She knew the shock was clear on her face. Did he usually stop to buy suspects dinner? She had so many questions but turned to Morris. "I'm sorry for your trouble. I hope the hearing goes well."

"Doubtful. Not the first time I got picked up."

"Oh, I see." The investigator portion of her was dying to ask what exactly he had repeatedly been picked up for.

"I steal things," said Morris and grinned.

"Morris," said the sheriff, his tone an admonition. "What did I say?"

"Let my lawyer do the talking?" said the boy.

"And?"

"Don't discuss the case."

Axel Trace nodded solemnly.

Morris turned to Rylee. "But I wasn't stealing for me this time. So that will be all right." He glanced to the sheriff for reassurance and received none.

Axel Trace looked as if he were taking his dog to the vet to be put down. His mouth tugged tight and his eyes… Were they glistening? His repeat blinking and the large swallow of soda he took seemed answer enough. Sheriff Trace cared for this boy.

Rylee choked down the rest of the burger in haste. Morris finished his sundae and grinned, smacking his lips in satisfaction. On closer inspection, he did not seem quite a boy but a man acting like a boy. He certainly didn't have a grip on the seriousness of his position. Why hadn't the information on Stanley Coopersmith included that he had a boy with special needs?

"How old are you, Morris?" she asked.

"Twenty." He showed a gap-toothed smile.

That was bad news. "I see."

She glanced to Trace, whose mouth went tight. Then she looked back to Morris. Her gaze slid to the sheriff.

He motioned to Morris with two fingers. "Come on, sport. Time to go."

Morris stood, towering over the sheriff by six inches. He was painfully thin. He wore neither handcuffs nor zip ties on his wrists. Trace pointed at his unit. Morris wadded up his paper wrappers and shot them basketball-style, as if hitting a foul shot. Then he cheered for his success and finally slipped into the passenger side of the sheriff's car.

"Is that wise? Having him up front with you?" she asked.

"Morris and I have an agreement."

Morris called from inside the cruiser. "Coke and comic for good behavior."

She stared at the young man and staunched the urge to open the door and release him.

"You have a good evening, Rylee."

"Thank you for the burger, Axel." The intentional use of his first name seemed all right. He'd used her given name first. But he just stood there, staring at her. And her breath was coming in short staccato bursts; she regretted dropping the distance of formality.

He gave her the kind of smile that twisted her heart and then returned to his duty, delivering a boy who should be entering a group home to the court systems.

Rylee headed back to her motel but then veered instead into the Walmart parking lot. It wasn't until she found herself in the books section that she realized she was looking at comics. The boy was spending the night in jail; he could at least have another superhero to keep him company.

Rylee made her purchase and used the GPS to find the jail in Kinsley. There, she was buzzed in and escorted back by a patrolman who allowed her to give Morris the graphic novel.

"You are a nice lady." Morris beamed. Then his voice held a note of chastisement. "Did you pay for this?"

She would have laughed if not faced with a boy who should not have been there in the first place.

Chapter Four

Observe and report. Rylee took her chief's directive to heart as she set off the next morning, the first Tuesday of September, to observe the next group on the watch list. The survivalists headed by Stanley Coopersmith. The group's rhetoric centered around surviving the apocalypse triggered by foreign terrorists. Ironic, as that scenario might turn out much more plausible than anyone in federal law enforcement had thought until a few months ago and the very reason she was here today.

It was hard to believe that such a group might aid foreign terrorists until you recalled your history and cult leader Charles Manson's attempts to begin a race war by murdering innocent affluent white victims, including Sharon Tate. It was terrifying, the lengths individuals might go to bring about their worldview.

At 7:00 a.m., Rylee left her car on the shoulder and hiked through the woods to a place where she could observe the central compound. Even though she was dressed all in earth colors for camouflage and was wearing a forest green wool sweater and a brown leather jacket atop her gray jeans and brown work boots with thick socks, she had underestimated the chill in the morning air. She had plenty of time to think about her inadequate wardrobe, among other things, as she lay on her belly in the pale green ferns. A cool September breeze shook the leaves overhead, sending down a cascade of yellow leaves through the fog.

"Should have worn a wool cap," she muttered to herself.

Maple leaves fluttered through the shafts of sunlight, giving hope that the fog would lift, as she watched the compound through binoculars. From this position, she had a clear line of sight to a large crumbling former dairy barn that might have once been yellow, two new prefab outbuildings with metal exteriors and roofs and a weathered farmhouse, looking patchy with the graying wood peeking out beneath flaking white paint.

One of the newer structures was a dock with a covered large boathouse on the St. Regis River that flowed into the St. Lawrence. That structure meant that it was reasonable to assume that the survivalists did leave their land. Did they use their boats to traffic in illegal drugs or human beings? Operations needed funding and she had yet to discover theirs. They were no longer farmers. That much was certain.

Had Stanley Coopersmith headed to court to defend his son?

Her reports on this group said that their leader never left the facility and his younger brothers, Joseph and Daniel, both married with children, rarely left their land. Stanley, who was married to Judy Coopersmith, had two grown boys—Edward, who they called "Eddie," and Morris, whom she had met on the night of her arrival.

She shivered with the cold as she counted occupants, noted physical descriptions into a digital recorder and snapped shots through her telephoto lens. As the morning stretched on and the sunlight finally reached her, she daydreamed about making a major arrest. Was it possible her runner had left Mohawk land? The Mohawk reservation land ended at the St. Regis River, just a short distance from Coopersmith's property. Had this been the runner's destination? The journey along would have been easy overland, or on the St. Lawrence River, with an escort of survivalists.

If she intercepted the shipment from Siming's Army, her boss would have to promote her. Then Rylee might ask for an assignment in New York City. What would her father think of that?

She sighed. Would he be proud?

The sound of a trigger's click dropped her from her daydreams like an acorn from an oak and made her stiffen. Her skin flushed hot and her fingers tingled. She held the binoculars; making a grab for her weapon seemed like suicide. Why hadn't she placed her weapon nearer to hand?

"Lace your fingers behind your head," came the order from a male voice behind her. The smell of the earth beneath her now turned her stomach and the ground seemed to churn as if heaved by an earthquake.

"Roll over," ordered her captor.

"I'm a federal agent. Homeland Security." For once, her voice did not shake.

There was a pause and then the command to roll over again.

She pushed off and rolled, coming to her seat. The

man holding a rifle was the brother of the family's leader—Daniel Coopersmith. She recognized him by his ginger beard and the scar across the bridge of his nose. He held the rifle stock pressed to his cheek and the barrel aimed at her chest.

"Stand up."

She released her laced fingers as she did so. The blood pounding through her veins made her skin itch. This might be her only chance to reach her weapon. Her only chance to avoid capture.

"Don't," he advised.

The roar in her ears nearly deafened her.

He wasn't taking her. That much she knew, because she was not creating a hostage situation on her first assignment. As she came upright, she swept her leg behind his and knocked him from his feet. As his arms jerked outward in reflex, she seized the barrel of the rifle and yanked. By the time Daniel recovered enough to scramble backward, she had his rifle pointed at him.

"It ain't loaded," he said.

She felt the weight of the firearm and gave him a look of disappointment.

"Daniel, have you had any visitors, other than me, recently?"

"What kind of visitors?"

"Smugglers."

"Anyone crosses our land we know it. Got cameras everywhere. How we spotted you."

"Your family likes their privacy?"

"We don't assist illegals if that's what you mean."

"Why is that?"

"They're carriers. Part of the scourge to come."

She knew the dogma.

"You know your nephew is in court this morning?" she asked.

Daniel curled his fingers around his beard and tugged.

"I knew he run off again. He get arrested?"

"Shoplifting."

"Comics again?"

She shrugged.

"Stan is gonna tan his hide."

"Not if he's in prison. Second offense."

Daniel seemed to forget she was pointing his rifle at him as he turned to go.

"I gotta go tell Judy." He glanced at her over his shoulder. "You best git. Leave my rifle on the road by your vehicle. That is if Stan don't already got your car."

"Stop." She had her weapon out and it *was* loaded.

He stopped and glanced back at her.

"You threatened a federal agent," she said to her retreating would-be opponent.

"I threatened a trespasser who's also an agent. We got constitutional rights. Illegal search. Illegal surveillance. Just cause. Illegal seizure." He continued speaking about rights and threats as he wound through the trees and out of sight.

She watched him go.

As it happened, when she reached her vehicle, she found Stanley Coopersmith waiting with his wife, Judy. Coopersmith was a man in his sixties, silver-haired, slim and muscular with a mustache that would have made any rodeo cowboy proud. His wife's hair was short and streaked with silver. She had the body of a woman accustomed to physical work and the lined face of a smoker.

Coopersmith did not move the rifle he held resting over his shoulder at her approach. She kept her personal weapon drawn but lowered.

"You holding my boy?"

"Sir, I'm Homeland Security—"

"We know who you are," said Judy Coopersmith, her chin now aimed at Rylee like a knife. "You holding my boy?"

"No, ma'am. Morris was arrested for shoplifting by local law enforcement. He has a hearing scheduled for this morning."

"You come here to tell us this?" said Coopersmith.

"No. I'm here investigating a case."

"You here to shut us down?"

Visions of Waco, Texas, flared like a dumpster fire in her mind.

"I am not. My job is to secure our borders."

"Well, we can assure you that this border is secure. Nobody sneaks through this patch of ground without us knowing. Yourself included."

"That's reassuring," said Rylee. "Has anyone tried recently?"

The two exchanged a look but did not reply. *No answer is still an answer*, she thought.

She took a leap of faith that their mutual threat made her, if not an ally, at least not an enemy. "We have intelligence that indicates something dangerous might be coming over from Canada. I'd ask you to be extra vigilant and hope that you will alert me if there is anything that threatens our national security."

Another long look blazed between the two.

"Why do you think we're up here?" asked Coopersmith. "Just a bunch of crazies playing war games in the woods? We know what's coming."

"And you do not think the federal government is capable of stopping threats from foreigners."

"If I did, why would I build a bunker?"

Rylee glanced toward her vehicle. "I'd best get back."

It was a long, long walk…to her vehicle. She did not draw an easy breath until she was safely behind the wheel. However, when she pressed the starter, her vehicle gave only an impotent click. The engine did not turn over on any of her next three attempts. There was no motor sound. In fact, the only sound was the thumping drumbeat of her heart.

THE FOG HAD settled into a steady drizzle by midday. Axel reached the stretch of old timber bordering Coopersmith land. He'd received a tip from Hal Mondello, who knew how to spot a fed's car if anyone alive did, that Rylee had headed past his place. Beyond Mondello land was the cult that called itself the Congregation of Eternal Wisdom. Beyond that was Hal Coopersmith's spread and his survivalist family. He didn't know which was a worse place for Rylee. For personal reasons, he decided to try Coopersmith's first and backtrack if necessary.

Hal Mondello was not a friend, but he protected his self-interest. Having the sheriff rein in a fed nosing around would be to his benefit. Hence, the call.

Mondello called himself a farmer, but everything he raised went into his cash crop, moonshine. Hal supplied most of the entire region with hard liquor. His brew was popular for its potency and the fact that it was cheap, due to Hal's complete avoidance of paying any federal tax. That made his moonshine a working man's favorite. Thankfully, that sort of violation fell under the auspices of the ATF, who had found his operation too small to be bothered with.

Axel raced out to the Coopersmiths' main gate, running silent, but exceeding the speed limit the entire way. He understood the Coopersmiths' desire to live off the grid, be largely self-sufficient, but he didn't understand living in a constant state of fear of some upcoming disaster from which only you and yours would survive. What kind of a world would that be, anyway? The thought of only Axel and his family surviving such a calamity gave him a shudder.

On the other hand, he did admire the Coopersmith family. Before they'd taken to their compound and ceased interacting with the outside world, Axel had been to their farm and respected the close-knit group. Anything could be taken too far. Religion came to his mind and he shuddered again.

He'd just be happy to have a family that didn't scare him so much that he didn't dare leave them out of his sight. And he owed Stanley Coopersmith for getting him out of his abysmal situation and helping him take his GED. Without him and Kurt Rogers, Axel didn't know where he might be now.

Axel was pleased to find Stanley's oldest son, Edward Coopersmith, minding the gate when he roared up. He and Eddie had enlisted in the army together and the two had been friends up until a year ago when his father had shut the family up on their land.

By the time Axel had left his sheriff's unit, the dust he'd raised was falling about them in a fine mist, settling on his hat and the hood of his car. Here, beneath the cover of trees, the drizzle had not succeeded in reaching.

He and his former comrade stood on opposite sides of a closed metal gate.

"Where is she, Eddie?"

"Who?"

"The homeland security agent your family is detaining."

Eddie could not meet his gaze.

"No concern of yours, I reckon."

"Eddie!"

His friend gripped the shoulder strap of the rifle slung over his shoulder so tightly his knuckles went bloodless.

"She's up at the farm," Eddie admitted.

"Under duress?"

"Not that I could see. But they was armed. So was she, come to that."

"Trespassing?"

"Well, she was."

"Eddie, she's a federal agent. You do not want her harmed."

His friend offered no reassurance.

"Bring me up."

"No outsiders."

"I'm not an outsider. I've eaten at your table. Your ma taught me algebra."

"Still…she ain't your concern."

Axel imagined the news crews and federal helicopters circling the compound. He had to stop this right now. Looking back, he didn't know why he did it. Perhaps because it was the only idea that popped into his head.

"She's my girl," said Axel.

"She's what now?" Eddie cocked his head.

Axel doubled down. "That's why she's up here, berry picking."

"With binoculars?"

"She's my fiancée and I won't have her touched."

"If she's your girl, why she up here alone?"

"Rylee is deciding if she wants to live up this way. I imagine she got…confused. Turned around."

"She was armed."

"Everyone up here is armed. We got bear and moose and elk." *And survivalists with semi-automatic assault rifles*, he finished silently.

Eddie released his grip on the rifle strap to scratch under his jaw at the coarse black beard. He looked so much different than from just a few years back when he was muscular and fit. Now his body looked undernourished and his face gaunt.

Axel watched Eddie as the man considered his options in silence.

After a long silent stretch, Axel had had about enough. "Open the gate or I'm ramming it."

"You can't do that." Their eyes met.

"I'm getting my girl so open up or stand aside."

Chapter Five

"Your girl, huh?" His old friend did little to hide his disappointment and Axel wondered if perhaps Eddie was attracted to Rylee. His answer came a moment later.

"She's very pretty. Kind of prickly, though."

"True on both accounts."

He realized that here on the compound, Eddie had little opportunity to meet eligible women. Rylee was a beauty and smart and he was certain she would have zero interest in locking herself up on nine hundred acres to wait for disaster.

Rylee was here to stop that impending doom from arriving. He admired her for that.

"Eddie, I'm getting in my vehicle. That gate best be open before I get there."

It wasn't a bluff. He knew that his modest yearly budget did not include major damage to his vehicle, but he was getting up to the farm. By the time he had his unit in drive, Eddie was swinging back the gate.

Axel paused just inside to speak to Eddie. "Why don't you come to my place for dinner one day?"

"Can't." Eddie made a face.

"Open invitation," he said and headed off. Axel

bounced along the twin groves that served as the access road to the compound, his windshield wipers screeching over the glass as he tried to clear the mist and mud.

RYLEE HAD BEEN stripped of her weapons and now accepted escort to one of the outbuildings. Judy Coopersmith had left her to see to her youngest son, Morris, who was heading to court today. Before leaving, she warned her husband, Stanley, that *this little gal is a guest and is to be treated like one.*

Stanley Coopersmith had his brother Joseph working on her car that had either a bad starter or a bad battery. Stanley thought Rylee should see something in his garage before leaving. She had time on her hands and so if Mr. Coopersmith wanted to give her a tour, she was happy to take it.

The garage turned out to be a huge prefab carport of aluminum, with a vertical roof that looked wide enough to park two tractor trailers in.

"We use it to repair our vehicles and construction. It's right in here."

The odor of motor oil, mildew and rust assaulted her before they'd cleared the single door that stood beside the huge twin garage doors. Inside, two pickup trucks stood end to end, one on blocks and the other with the hood open and a greasy tarp draped over one side.

Beside these casualties sat a backhoe with the bucket removed and showing one broken tooth. Along the back was a long tool bench. She picked her way past various replacement parts that littered the grease-stained concrete. On the cluttered surface of the tool bench sat one pristine device. It was a drone—white, approximately thirty-four inches with eight rotors, one of which had been damaged. She glanced at Coopersmith, who motioned her forward.

"Go on," he said.

"Where did this come from?"

"Darned if I know, but I took that shot. It was carrying something, like a duffel bag. It dropped it across the river before I made that shot. Crashed out back and we scooped it up."

"What's across the river?" she asked.

He looked startled. "That's the Mohawk Nation."

"Do you believe that it is theirs?"

"No saying. I didn't shoot it until it was over my place."

"And its cargo?"

"Dropped on the Kowa side of the river."

"Did they retrieve what the drone was carrying?"

"Can't say. But I know someone has been trying to activate that drone remotely."

"How do you know that?"

"Because the damn thing keeps moving around the garage. It's why I chained her down."

Rylee used a cloth to lift the drone. "Heavy."

"Thirty pounds and no serial number. No markings at all that I can see."

"When did you find it?"

"Yesterday."

Monday, she realized, and the same day that Border Patrol followed a small man dropped off on the Canadian side, who crossed the border through a wooded area and then fled onto Mohawk land carrying a duffel bag. Had their suspect had the drone to carry out the cargo or did he have outside help?

"Were you planning to report it?"

"No. I was planning to take it apart and keep it. But if you want it, I'll accept offers."

"Offers?" She did a poor job holding back her surprise. "How much?"

"Take five hundred for it."

"Done."

She reached for her wallet, zipped in her blazer.

"You carry that much?"

She nodded, opening the billfold.

"Should have asked for six," he said.

"I'll give you seven." And she did.

Stanley accepted the cash.

"Has this happened before?"

"Trespassers? Sure. Just today, for instance." He gave her a pointed look and she flushed as he continued on. "But drones. That's a new one for me."

A voice came from behind the pickup.

"Pop?"

"Back here."

Edward Coopersmith appeared, red-faced and unable to make eye contact with her. Behind him came Sheriff Trace. He had no trouble making eye contact and the result was an instant acceleration of her heartbeat. The physical reaction to this man was getting bothersome. She scowled at the pair as they continued toward them.

"Axel, what a surprise." Stanley offered his hand to Trace and cast a scowl at his son.

"I wouldn't have brung him, but this here is his gal and he's worried."

Stanley looked from Axel, whose jaw was locked tight, to Rylee, whose mouth swung open.

"Interesting news, seeing she's only been here a day and a half."

Edward glared at Axel, who shrugged.

Stanley Coopersmith spoke again. "We aren't detaining her, Axel. Fact, she's leaving anytime. You want to give her a lift?"

"I'll need my weapons," said Rylee.

"'Fraid our policy is to confiscate the firearms of trespassers."

"And my vehicle?"

"Also confiscated."

"It was on a county road."

"The road belongs to the county. The land is ours. You left the government land when you left the road."

"Taking a federal vehicle might be a problem for you," said Rylee.

Coopersmith did not blink. She looked to the damaged drone, itching to get it to her people. A glance at Trace told her he was worried. He motioned with his head toward the exit.

Rylee looked to Coopersmith. "What do you want for them?"

"Money is good."

"What about shotgun shells? I have ten boxes in my trunk."

"You don't anymore."

Here, Axel stepped in, looping an arm around her waist and cinching her tight. Her side pressed against his and even though their skin never touched, her body tingled with awareness and she temporarily lost the ability to speak. His scent enveloped her. He smelled of pine soap and leather.

"I appreciate you looking out for my girl, Mr. Coopersmith. And for all you did for me when I was a boy. I'd appreciate you allowing us safe passage through your land."

"Very fact she's up here shows I'm right. It's coming. I feel it in my bones."

Rylee glanced to Trace to see what *it* might be. His hand rested familiarly on her hip and she found it harder to think as her body pressed to his.

"What about two cases of MREs for your trouble?" he offered, referring to the military Meals Ready to Eat. The food staple stored for years and he thought might just appeal to a man ready to hide in a bunker.

"I'll take six for the drone and safe passage off our lands."

"And her vehicle, weapons and anything else you took from her car."

"Done."

Axel released her to shake on the deal. Rylee stepped away from both men and headed toward the door.

She resented being bargained for like a milk cow. But she said nothing. Safely clear of Axel's embrace, her mind began functioning again. She retrieved the drone and carried it with her as they left the garage.

Edward hovered by her opposite side. "If things don't work out for you two, you could give me a call."

She blinked at the strange offer. "You have phones out here?"

"No, but Axel can get a message to me."

Axel chose this moment to press a hand to her lower

back. The gesture was intimate. "We best be on our way, sweetheart."

The endearment sounded forced but made Edward flinch. Inexplicably, she felt a tightening in her throat and her breath came in tiny gasps. She forced her mouth closed and breathed through her nose all the way to her vehicle, parked before the main house.

There, she watched her weapons loaded back in her trunk. Everything went back in place except the shot-gun shells. She placed the drone on top and accepted the keys from Stanley.

"You understand this is a one-time deal on account of my wife saying you was to be treated as a guest."

"Do you always ransom your guest's belongings?"

Stanley Coopersmith's smile was wily. "Generally, I just keep them."

"You will have to notify me if you apprehend or spot any more trespassers or see any unusual activity."

"Actually, I don't have to." Stanley accepted her card.

Axel held open her door and cast her an impatient look. Those gray-blue eyes relayed messages that she could not decipher other than his impatience and a pos-sible brewing storm.

Rylee allowed Axel to walk her alongside of the sedan and tuck her into her seat as if she were a child unable to successfully open or close a car door. Then she followed his vehicle off the property and out of a gate that was the only gap in a perimeter fence that stretched into the woods in either direction.

A chill now lifted the hairs on her arms and neck. Had Stanley actually been considering ransoming her? She was a federal agent and taking her hostage would have brought the FBI straight to his property line. There, federal authorities would have waited during negotiations that she realized might have stretched on and on. For the first time, her annoyance with Axel turned to the realization that she might just owe him her thanks. If that situation had escalated, the ramifications could have been disastrous for all parties.

Axel had gotten her out of a survivalist camp without bloodshed, quickly and with only the merest gesture of a bargain. Just the dashboard computer was worth far more than a few cases of prepackaged food and shotgun shells.

That was twice now he'd pulled her fanny from the fire. Rylee gripped the wheel as she followed Axel onto the highway and back toward Kinsley. Perhaps a collaboration with the locals was not just some empty gesture and words from her department. She might get farther with his help if she included him in her investigation and, perhaps, keep custody of her car.

Trouble was she didn't trust him. All she really knew was that he was a local guy, generally liked, with an impressive military career that he had left to come here. His background information was general at best. But where had he been before he was fostered to Kurt Rogers at age thirteen? And what had happened to make him leave the army shortly after his fatal shooting of fellow servicemen?

As an army brat, she didn't approve of his taking the early discharge option. Her father, sister and brothers were all career Marine Corp so she shared her father's aversion for the army.

"One way to get to know someone is to speak to them," she said to the car's interior.

Rylee was not a joiner. An introvert by nature, she was comfortable only with her siblings, and some more than others. They were nearly back to Kinsley before her phone picked up cellular service. She used the vehicle's communication system to call her boss.

Someone from the Glens Falls office would pick up the drone. Hopefully, they could glean some information from the navigation system. She'd seen her share of drones during professional training and recognized this one was not the garden-variety hobbyist craft. Too sophisticated and too expensive for the average operator.

By the time she reached her motel, she realized she had missed lunch and was starving. In the motel lot, the sheriff peeled off to park in the guest area. She checked the drone in the trunk. It was not in the spot she had placed it and there were scrape marks on the inner surface of the trunk. The blades began to whir, and she slammed the trunk closed.

This was a safer spot to hold the device than the motel room and she wasn't sure she could get it in there without it getting away. She glanced around. You usually had to be within sight of a drone to effectively operate it. This sort might have a longer range and all sorts of navigational upgrades.

Axel was beside her car as she locked the vehicle.

"You know, I do have other things to do besides collect you from private property."

She turned and met him with a bright smile. "And I appreciate your efforts and I'd like to take you out to lunch as a thank-you."

It was as if she'd frozen him in some tractor beam. He stood with his mouth half open, a finger raised to continue his lecture, and now seemed unsure how to proceed.

She closed her hand around his extended index finger and lowered his hand to his waist. He frowned before drawing his hand back. She doubted he intended the action of gliding his digit from her closed palm to be sexual, but from the startled gaze and the drop of her stomach, the friction had done just that.

He stood speechless, and she was finding a lack of oxygen in this corner of the parking lot. *Oh, no*, she thought. Not this one. He's overbearing and judgmental. He's in a dead-end career at the top of the world. She had the impression he played fast and loose with the law and enforced only the regulations that fell under his auspices. But those blue-gray eyes. They reminded her of a winter sky. Axel lifted his hands and for a moment she thought he would hold her again. The little show for Coopersmith replayed in her mind with the firm feel of his fit body.

She stepped closer. He grasped her shoulders and for just a second he seemed unsure if he should push or pull. Rylee leaned toward him and he extended his arms, sending her back a step.

"Separate cars. You follow me," he said and whirled away. His retreat came as close to a jog as a man could manage and still be walking. She'd never seen someone in such a hurry to be rid of her.

It only then occurred to her that the sheriff might be as hesitant of her as she was of him.

Her hands went to her hips. "We'll see about that."

Chapter Six

Axel checked the rearview every ten seconds to be sure that Rylee was following him. His heart was thumping as if he had run all the way to Bear Creek Café. He tried and failed to convince himself he was just anxious that she not veer off to find herself in another jam that required an extraction.

But it was a lie. He wanted her in his arms again. That little stunt for the benefit of the Coopersmiths had been a mistake. He'd been close enough to smell the light floral scent of her hair and feel the fit of her body against his. Both made him hungry for far more than lunch.

He realized, with a sinking feeling, that he was spending so much time minding her business because she was so appealing. Even her false bravado came across as charming. He groaned aloud as he set his blinker tapping and made a slow turn into the lot. Rylee was parked and out of her car before he even had his turned off.

"Fast woman," he muttered.

He tried to hold the door for her, but she made it inside unassisted and told Bonnie they'd prefer a booth. Then she took the one farthest from the counter.

"Waitresses have ears like elephants," she told him as she slid into her side and used a napkin from the metal dispenser to send the crumbs from the last patron's meal onto the floor.

She sat to give herself a clear view of her vehicle out the window.

Smart, he thought. *Keep an eye on that drone.*

Bonnie followed them back with menus and a wet cloth to finish the job Rylee had started.

"Drinks?" Bonnie said, grinning broadly at Axel as she wiggled her eyebrows at him.

His scowl only made her smile broaden. Bonnie was short and round and the pink apples of her cheeks seemed more responsible than her nose for keeping her owlish glasses in place. Her hair was blond, short and starched straight as the rails on a fence. She stood on tiny feet, balancing her girth with the skill of an acrobat.

"Iced tea," said Rylee, flipping the laminated menu over and over as if something new might appear.

Bonnie didn't ask Axel what he wanted but did pause to give him a "what's her deal?" look before departing. She returned a moment later with black coffee and Rylee's iced tea.

Axel removed his jacket and set it beside him in the booth. They ordered—a burger with fries for her, an egg salad sandwich with fresh fruit for him. She lifted her brow at his choice but said nothing.

"Any news from your home office?" he asked.

"None that I can discuss."

"They coming for the drone?"

"Of course."

She glanced out the window as a line of bikers roared past, rattling the window.

"They part of the North Country Riders group?" she asked, making the question seem casual.

The fact that she knew not only that they had a motorcycle gang—or "club," as they self-identified—up here but also their name did not bode well.

"How you know of them?"

"Briefings. They bring weed over the border. How is up for debate. You made any arrests in that department?" She sounded as if she already knew the answer and did not approve. He switched from wanting to kiss her to wanting to ditch her.

"Smuggling is your department. Best leave the borders to BP boys and ICE, right?" he said, referring to Border Patrol and Immigration and Customs Enforcement, the two branches of Homeland Security working on drug enforcement up here.

"Not if they sell it in your county," she countered.

"They don't."

"So it just passes through here like the water through the aquifer?"

"More like the St. Lawrence. What travels past us and down state isn't my concern."

"Maybe it should be."

"You have no idea what I do up here all day. Do you?"

"Eat barbecue and gamble at the casino?" she guessed.

"I cover up to thirty calls a day. Mostly folks who smeared themselves and their vehicles all over our roads. Drunk drivers, texting drivers, sleepy and distracted drivers and then we have the domestic violence calls, drunk and disorderly, and you might not be surprised to hear that most of those last ones are guests on vacay. But the winters up here are hard, lonely, and we have suicides. I also accompany Child Protective Services and they are way too busy here." He took a sip of coffee, burned his tongue and quickly chased the brew with ice water.

"You okay?"

"I will be when you head back down to Glens Falls."

"You got a particular reason you want me gone?" That one sounded like an accusation.

"You insinuating I'm dirty?"

"Just that you work up here without much supervision."

"I'm supervised by the town council and elected by the citizens I serve."

"Eloquent." She pursed her lips and his blood surged in all the wrong places.

Truth was, just sitting this close made his nerves jangle like a jar full of quarters rolling along the floor.

"Anything else?" she asked.

"I don't like your brand of cooperation."

"How's that?"

"The kind where you expect me to assist in an investigation of which I have no information."

She sat back and folded her arms. Her posture said that she wasn't interested in any sort of cooperation. Then, unexpectedly, her arms dropped to her sides and she leaned in until her torso pressed to the edge of the table. He leaned in as well, close enough to smell her skin and the spicy, earthy scent of something that seemed wildly erotic. His fingers, resting on his knees, curled, wadding the fabric of his trousers in his fists, and he told himself to sit back. But he didn't.

"All you need to know is that I am searching for illegal border crossings."

"You looking for a person or what they carry?"

"Both."

The lines on her face told him the rest.

"It's soon?"

"Any time."

"So why you?"

"Why not me?"

"You clearly don't have experience in the field. Either that or your method of investigation is to piss everyone off. Are you trying to rattle them into doing something stupid?"

Her chin lifted and she said nothing. But her cheeks blazed, indicating to him that her technique was no ploy. The high color bloomed on her throat and the vee of skin visible above her buttoned-up blouse. His blood sizzled and turned to ash.

"I volunteered." She clasped her drink between both hands, lacing her fingers around the glass. "Most of my department is assigned elsewhere."

He pictured the briefing and this county being mentioned and her hand shooting in the air. She wasn't up to it. Now he felt irritated at her supervisors for sending her and annoyed that he'd have to babysit her during her little field trip.

"Were you that kid with her hand in the air, asking if there was homework?"

The flush bloomed brighter. "Homework is important." She cleared her throat. "This assignment is important."

"If that's true, why send you up here all alone?"

"Who said I'm alone?"

Did she have contacts, informants or undercover agents up here? He tried to think of any new arrivals. But the fall season brought many visitors to watch the leaves turn and boat on the St. Lawrence.

"Still, if this were a likely place for your illegal border jumpers, I'd expect a higher presence."

She conceded the point with a slight incline of her head. "Intel indicates that this crossing will be at the other end of the state."

"Buffalo?"

"Most likely. But this area is still a possibility."

"How possible?"

"Least likely, according to the analysts' report."

"So they sent you in the opposite direction of trouble. That about it?" In other words, her department was trying to get rid of her. He had a few thoughts of his own on why. Where he came from they called that a snipe hunt.

He waited for an answer.

She glanced away.

"I see." He hadn't meant that to sound so insulting. But it had.

Rylee sat back as if she'd slapped him. The arms came up and around her chest again. Her face hardened, and her eyes went cold as frozen ground.

"I know it can be difficult, having federal involvement in your county."

No use holding back. He laid it out there. "You're

what's difficult. And I'm guessing that is exactly why they sent you up here. Not the most popular agent down there in Glens Falls. Am I right?"

"From my perspective, I'm thorough."

He continued to stare, and she glanced away.

"You can rub folks wrong."

She nodded, forcing a smile that struck him as sad. She was the know-it-all in the office. Least popular because she was often right. And she had the social skills of a bull shark.

So why did he feel the need to help her?

"You could get better cooperation if you turned down the aggression a notch."

The arms slid back to her sides and she clasped her hands before her on the table. Her perfectly shaped pink nails with the white French tips tapped restlessly. She eased back into the vinyl seat. Their eyes met and a chill danced over his skin.

"I wanted a field assignment and I got one. I'll admit that I don't play well with others. Abrasive and dictatorial were the words my supervisor used just before shipping me up here."

"I can see that. I might have said headstrong." He sipped his coffee, now just the right temperature to scald his throat without leaving any permanent damage. "Thank you for telling me all that."

"I'm sure you are even more anxious to see my back than she was."

He lowered his chin. "No, I think your analysis might be wrong."

Her eyes lit up and looked at him as if for the first time.

"Were you sent here, or did you choose to come here?" he asked.

"I chose because I think the analysis is wrong. This border is a strong possibility."

"But the boss went with the numbers and was happy to let you take a field trip."

She puffed out her cheeks and blew away a breath. He waited and at last she said, "Yes."

"How big a load?"

Her brows rose and studied him. Judged him, he thought. Then she shook her head.

No details for the sheriff, he realized.

"I'd like to ask you about some of the organizations in your county."

The path between them was back to a one-way road, he realized. She didn't trust him, and he wasn't sure if that was standard or if she had something on him. The obvious reared up inside him like a jab to his belly. How thorough had her research been before her arrival?

He studied her and decided she likely knew it all. He sank down in the booth seat, bracing his hands on either side of him so they acted like flying buttresses to the cathedral.

She continued, all business again, "The Kowa Mohawks are on my watch list because of their known smuggling activities."

"Cigarettes."

"What?"

"They buy in Canada and sell on their reservation and skip the federal tobacco tax."

"They transport merchandise through New York State without declaring them. It's trafficking."

"I guess they figure that since they are a sovereign nation, they don't pay income tax."

"Sovereign nations don't import goods over federal and state highways."

"They have land on both sides of the St. Lawrence and all this land was theirs once."

"Agree to disagree," she said.

"Okay."

She made a face. "I don't want to win the argument. I want you to understand that some of their members are radical in ideology and could, conceivably, be convinced to assist in a domestic attack."

"Not buying it. I've never seen them bringing in more than smokes. Next?"

"The North Country Riders?"

He nodded. The motorcycle gang did a lot worse than smuggling tobacco. They carried weed from Canada into New York. They also carried illegal pharmaceuticals.

"Possibly. For the right price, I believe they'd carry anything or anyone."

"The Mondellos?"

"Moonshiners? They are all about avoiding taxation and the feds. That family has been in business since prohibition."

"They have property directly on the river, facilitating their illegal distribution. They have the means and the opportunity."

"Motive?"

"Same as for the booze. Money."

He shrugged. "I can't rule them out. Who else?"

"The Coopersmith family. Survivalists are one thing,

but what if they feel it is necessary to give the coming Armageddon a little shove?"

"I've known them since I was a boy. They are all about protecting their own, protecting this country. I can't see them doing anything to jeopardize either. Who else?"

"That's it." Her eyes still twinkled, and he felt for all the world like he was in an interrogation room. Sitting here, under the guise of helping her out when actually he was on her little list. She knew. He was convinced. But some tiny part of him did not want to say it aloud.

He shook his head. "You left out the congregation."

"A religious order?" she said, but her eyes narrowed as if just considering them.

He shifted in his seat, realized he was relaying his discomfort and forced himself to sit still.

"You know about them?"

"Some." She gave nothing away.

"They are also on the St. Regis River, between the Mondellos and the Coopersmiths, just a stone's throw from the St. Lawrence."

"That's true."

"Father Wayne heads the outfit. Call themselves the Congregation of Eternal Wisdom." He waited for her eyes to light up with recognition or her brows to lower in disapproval. But instead, her expression remained open.

"Go on," she said.

He didn't want to. The coffee now sloshed in his stomach like waves tossed by an angry sea. This storm's origin came from deep within himself, out of the sight of his DHS observer. Funny how something that had been his entire world for so many years, to her, meant nothing at all.

"It's a cult. They call themselves a congregation but it's a cult. They also live in a fenced compound. You might see some of the men outside the complex. They wear simple clothing. The top is a brown tunic. Bottom is baggy pants. No pockets, just a satchel, if they need to carry anything. Their heads are shaved and most wear beards."

"I haven't seen anyone like that. Is it an all-male order?"

He dropped his gaze to his half-finished coffee. "No. But you won't see the women. They stay put."

"Are they a radical group?"

"No. But their ideas are untraditional. Their leader says he is preparing them for ascension. They consider themselves the chosen and they consider children communal property."

"Many cultures share in raising children."

The small hairs on his neck lifted. "These kids don't know which of the women is their birth mother."

Now she was frowning but her notebook was out.

"They practice polygamy and some of the males undergo voluntary castration."

She stiffened. "What? Why?"

"Preparation for the afterlife. No sex there, according to Father Wayne. You'll know which ones have done this because they shave all their hair away." Axel lifted his mug and swallowed, tasting the remains of the coffee mingled with bitter memories. He should tell her the reverend's last name, but he just couldn't summon the courage.

"They sound like the Branch Davidians," she said.

"Except for the UFOs."

She sat back, leaving the pad open on the table. "Are you pulling my leg?"

He wished that were so. Axel pressed the flat of his palm to his middle, trying to settle his stomach.

"No joke. They live, farm, sing and dance out there on the river. And their leader has twisted theories of UFO visitations with God and scripture. The jumble is confusing but the gist is that reported alien visitations are actual angels sent by God in preparation for the end of the world. Only they call it the Rising."

"How many?"

"Hard to get an exact count. Thirty adults, maybe."

"How many children?"

"Social services go out there to check on them. The cult won't let kids be inoculated or register their births. They're homeschooled, or they tell us they are." He knew that schooling included creationism, their version of scripture and little else. "They collect the necessary textbooks and fill in all the correct paperwork." He locked his jaw so tight there was a distortion in his hearing, so he eased up.

"How do they fund their order?"

"Selling books and junk online. Taking donations and offering religious retreats. They recruit from the guests and once you are in, everything you own becomes theirs. Communal property."

"How do you know so much about them?"

Because I was born there.

"It's my business to know who lives in my county."

She lifted her pen and began writing. "I'll check them out."

And then she'd discover exactly where he came from.

"If you are going out there, you need me along."

"I don't."

"Rylee, trust me. You won't get past the gate without me. Let me help you."

She held his gaze and he held his breath.

"All right. I won't go out there without you."

Chapter Seven

On the third night in Onutake County, Rylee roared into the lot of the roadhouse favored by the North Country Riders on a red Harley Low Rider. The neon advertising for various beers sent colorful light gleaming across the chrome on the line of Harleys parked in a neat row along the front of the establishment, including the handicapped spots.

She parked her motorcycle at the end of the line of bikes and walked it back in preparation for a quick getaway that she hoped would not be necessary. Once the sled was leaning on its stand, Rylee tugged off the helmet and braced it under one arm, keeping her gun hand free.

She had prepared for her meet with the undercover agent from DHS stationed up here, dressing in clothing appropriate for a roadhouse in the territory of the North Country Riders. The tan slacks were tapered so she wore her calf-hugging suede boots over them. Her suede-fringed top covered all her assets and her brown leather jacket covered her service weapon. Under her bike helmet, she wore a black woolen cap.

She paused to take in her surroundings. Or was she just stalling?

That thought sent her forward, as she wondered again if she should have called the sheriff to request backup.

"It's just a meet. Make contact and get out." She tugged the wool cap lower over her ears, hoping to hide the most obvious of attributes, her blond hair.

No disguising she was female, because of her height. The longer she stood, the faster her heart beat.

"Did you ask for this field assignment or not?" she scolded. Despite the lecture, she suddenly missed her desk and her data with the kind of wistful longing usually reserved for departed friends.

Squaring her shoulders, she marched to the door, paused and then reached for the handle. The interior stank of stale beer and the thumping beat of music assaulted her eardrums. She swept the groups of occupants, seeing that the motorcycle gang occupied most of the tables and the area of the bar closest to that seating. There was a stage at the opposite side with a band playing '80s metal. No one seemed to be paying any attention to them as they shouted in each other's ears and tipped long-necked bottles back.

She made for the area of the bar closest to the band, farthest from the bikers and closest to the spot the servers picked up their orders for the tables.

The sticky floor made it seem she was walking across a surface slathered with glue. She set her helmet on the scarred surface of the bar, beside the heart someone had scratched into it.

As she waited to order, she busied herself looking for her contact. She did not know her, but Rylee's image had been sent to the agent. She still had five minutes to go before the meet.

Reaching into her coat pocket for her mace, she made sure it was close at hand. Then she retrieved her mobile phone and glanced at it because the screen showed she had made a call, connected and had been connected for three minutes. Had her helmet made the call?

She glanced at the caller information and groaned. Sheriff Axel Trace. Rylee lifted the phone to her ear but could hear nothing.

"Trace?" she asked.

"Rylee? Where are you? I was just having your phone geolocated."

"I'm fine. Sorry. Must have pocket dialed you."

"Fine? What's that music?"

"'Bye, Trace. I have to go."

"Rylee, where—" She disconnected and shoved the phone back in her pocket.

"What'll ya have?" The bartender was young with a bushy beard that did not disguise how painfully thin he was, or cover the tattoos on one side of his throat. It seemed to be a wing and the word *blessed*. The tips of the wing flew up behind his ear, which sported a plug the size of a nickel. Above his eyebrow was a musical note.

She ordered what most of the patrons were drinking.

"Glass or bottle?"

"Bottle."

The beer arrived and her server made a nice show of flipping the opener before uncapping the bottle and sliding it across the marred surface.

"What you riding?" he asked.

"Harley. 2016 Low Rider."

"Sweet."

A woman across the bar at the table extracted herself from the lap of a big man with a stomach that left her little room. She knew him. He was Lloyd Fudderman, head of the North Country Riders. But Rylee did not know that woman. The brunette wore a black T-shirt modified with a slice down the center to expose the tops of her breasts and so short her stomach and navel hardware were in full view. She strode away, swinging her hips to the delight of Fudderman, whose full salt-and-pepper mustache lifted on both sides of his mouth. His beard was stained yellow from tobacco, Rylee assumed, and his black leather vest showed various patches.

His woman wore unlaced biker boots and jeans that had been artfully torn and frayed across the knees and thighs. Her long wavy hair bounced with the rest of her as she passed behind Rylee to the bathrooms.

The lightbulb went off in her head at last and she slapped her money on the table, retrieved her helmet and beer and headed to the toilet. That must be her contact.

Rylee passed through the swinging door and into the brightly lit bathroom. At the row of sinks, a heavy-set bottle blonde uncapping a lipstick. The T-shirt she wore indicated that she was one of the staff. The young woman had a florid face that clashed with the lipstick she reapplied. The color of the cosmetic reminded Rylee of a dog's tongue. Rylee's contact was nowhere in sight. Rylee dipped to see under one of the two stalls and spotted the brunette's unlaced boots. She glanced to the employee, who eyed her in the mirror and then broke contact to check her phone.

Rylee's contact emerged, checked her hair and ignored the soap, sink and bottle blonde as she refastened her belt, which unfortunately sported a Rebel flag. Then she glanced at Rylee, scowled and headed out.

Rylee blinked after her in surprise.

"Agent Hockings?" asked the blonde.

Rylee opened her mouth and just managed to keep it from swinging open as she nodded.

"I'm Agent Beverly Diel."

"Yes," she managed, cocking her head as her entire system misfired. "Hello."

"That was Queeny. She's Fudderman's woman, though she's half his age. Seems to be a lot of that going around up here."

"In the gang?"

"And at the cult. Fudderman has been in contact with the head of the Congregation of Eternal Wisdom. You know them?"

"No."

"I haven't been able to contact any of the women out there and the men don't come in here or speak to secular women. I suggest you find out what you can about them. But do not go out to their assembly alone."

"Why not?"

"Because it's a cult. The headman has them all twisted up into believing they're the chosen people and the judgment is coming. They live separately, and they might be armed against what they see as a coming apocalypse. If you go, go with backup."

"I'll do that." She didn't have backup and wouldn't get any without first showing something to prove she was on the right track.

Beverly gave her a hard look.

"I won't."

"All right, then." She washed her hands and yanked down a paper towel from the dispenser with both hands.

"Did you get my report?"

She rolled her eyes. "Thin in evidence, heavy on speculation."

"I'm an analyst."

"I get that." The woman scanned Rylee's outfit, making her words seem like insults. "What I don't get is why you are up here instead of at your computer terminal."

"It was in my report."

"Rylee—" Her tone was one you used to explain to someone dim-witted. "You're fishing, am I right? Trying to get the attention of the supervisors who are ignoring you?"

"My report—"

"I read your personal file. You don't belong here. You don't have the training or the experience. Go home."

Rylee felt like a swimmer preparing to let go and sink into the deep.

"What do you think will happen if I call your supervisor?"

Rylee felt her skin grow cold and a shiver of fear inched up her spine. It wasn't the prospect of losing her job that frightened. It was the prospect of telling her father that she had lost her job that really made her gut twist.

But what if she were right? There was no turning back. She went home and admitted that she went rogue or she finished this and stopped this threat. Rylee narrowed her eyes, preparing to fight.

Beverly's brows lifted and she looked interested for the first time.

"The man who evaded Border Patrol…"

"The man you followed onto Kowa land?"

Her head dropped.

"Yeah. That's something."

Rylee lifted her gaze to meet Beverly's. The woman no longer seemed harmless. There was something of the hunter flashing in her dark eyes.

"He got away clean because someone from Fudderman's group picked him up. Took him back over the border, what I heard."

"What about his cargo?"

"Missing. The Kowa took it and that's all Fudderman's guys know."

"Did you report this?"

Her mouth went tight, and she gave Rylee a "what do you think?" look.

"So, they *do* carry illegals," Rylee said.

"First I've heard. It's been all weed and Oxy, so far as I can tell. I'm a regular buyer."

"I thought they didn't sell up here."

"Ha," she laughed.

Clearly, the sheriff did not know this. Or did he? It wouldn't be the first time a law enforcement officer had been paid to look the other way.

"What if I can get the cargo from the Kowa?"

Agent Diel cast a look that told Rylee she had no confidence that would happen, but then she gave her a patronizing smile and nodded.

"Sure, hon. You do that. But don't come back here dressed like that."

"Like what?"

"Like a magazine version of how tough girls dress." She shook her head as she scanned her from head to toe. "You see anyone in her wearing suede boots?"

"I came on a motorcycle."

"Every last one of them already knows you are here and who you are and what you are investigating. You'll get no help from that crew," said Diel.

"They running their own organization?"

"I don't know yet. Might find out in time. Now ride it out of here and don't come back. I'll contact you if I have anything."

"My number?"

Her face twisted and she lifted her phone. "I have it."

"So you could have called," asked Rylee.

"Wanted to get a look at you. Worse than I thought," she said. Then she capped her lipstick and shoved it in her front pocket before pausing at the door. "You should keep that outfit for Halloween. Maybe add a temporary tattoo."

Beverly left and the door banged shut.

Rylee braced herself on the counter, allowing her head to drop. When she opened her eyes, it was to see the tile comet—a streamer of toilet paper—fixed to the heel of one suede boot.

The commotion outside brought her up and to full alert.

The music had stopped and there was shouting coming from beyond the door. She recognized one voice. Axel Trace was bellowing her name.

Chapter Eight

Dressed in plain clothing tonight, Axel appreciated how quickly his presence inside the roadhouse had been noticed. The jeans, boots and flannel shirt beneath the open canvas jacket did nothing to keep him from being as recognizable as a roast pig at a vegan picnic. *Probably just as welcome, too*, he thought.

The patrons gradually came to rest, pivoting in their seats to face him as all conversation came to a halt. The band caught on last. First, the drummer lost the beat and then the bass player missed the bridge. The singer and lead guitarist opened his eyes, straightened and stepped back from the microphone. Feet shifted uneasily as the gathering cast glances from Fudderman and then back to him.

Fudderman lifted his half-finished longneck to his lips and tipped the bottle, draining the rest. Then he set the bottle down with a heavy crack that made the woman on his lap startle.

He pushed her off and to her feet, eyes never leaving Axel's. A smile came slowly to his lips as he sat back, relaxed, with one hand on his knee and the other on the bottle.

"Evening, Sheriff." He had the courtesy to not ask if the sheriff was lost or crazy, which Axel appreciated. "The fed is in the bathroom."

Axel glanced toward the dark alcove past the bar. Then he headed that way. A big man with a shaved head stepped before him, bringing Axel up short.

"Get out," he said, leaning in so Axel could smell his breath, stale with beer and raw onions.

"That your sled parked in the handicapped spot, Hooter?"

"You and I going to have a problem?"

"I won't. But you have a hundred-and-fifty-dollar fine for parking there."

"The hell you say." He began a string of obscenities that involved at least three suggestions that Axel perform physical impossibilities on himself. Then Hooter reached back for a bottle and began an arching swing toward Axel's head.

Axel kicked out Hooter's feet from beneath him. Top-heavy and drunk was a bad combination in a bar fight. Hooter went down hard. The smaller man who Axel didn't know jumped in, swinging a bottle. It was like being back on base in Germany on any Saturday night. Axel grabbed his attacker's wrist and drew back one finger, causing his opponent to scream as the finger dislocated. Unfortunately, he also dropped the bottle, which bounced off Axel's forehead before shattering on the ground.

"Rylee! Time to go! Rylee!" Axel shouted toward the women's bathroom as Hooter scrambled to his feet. He didn't get all the way up before Axel brought his knee to the man's gut, sending him to his hands and knees on the beer-soaked floor.

The men at the bar closed in, forming an ever-decreasing circle.

"Rylee! Get out here." Still time if she made a quick appearance.

She did, only she had her gun drawn. This brought the other occupants of the bar to their feet. Weapons of all sizes and types were drawn in response.

"You," said Rylee, pointing her weapon at the smaller man with the dislocated thumb. "Back up, now."

Her voice was cold and her demeanor terrifying. She seemed born for this, with a steady hand, calm control and chilling expression of anticipation.

The man backed up, cradling his finger. Hooter reached his feet with the help of a bar stool that he scaled like a child on a jungle gym.

The circle widened as Rylee stepped beside him.

"Which one hit you?" she asked.

Ah, she was going to defend him. He was touched. But he also wasn't crazy.

"Let's go," he said, heading toward the door.

Rylee backed along beside him, her pistol deterring any from closing in.

Outside, she lowered her weapon and faced him. "Where's your personal weapon?"

"I'm off duty."

They kept moving, her keeping an eye on the closed door to the bar and coming up short as he reached his vehicle. His sheriff's department SUV lay just beyond where he had parked it, only now it sat on its side, driver's door up.

"What the…" His words trailed off. He rounded on Rylee. "I'm done babysitting you."

"Who asked you?"

"You called me from this…this gang hangout and tell me you're fine."

"I was fine until you started screaming."

"I wasn't screaming."

The door behind them banged open and members of the North Country Riders spilled out like floodwater.

"Come on," she said tugging him toward the back side of the bar. He followed, keeping pace as she jogged along.

Behind them, shouts and the sound of beer bottles smashing on the pavement urged them to greater speeds.

"I'm on the other side," she said, leading the way to a Harley Low Rider.

He paused, agog, forgetting everything as he admired the bike, which was all black right down to the fork and tailpipes.

"Wow."

She straddled the seat, righted the bike and rolled it forward off the kickstand. She'd parked the Harley for a quick escape. He eyed the rear seat that was higher and smaller than the saddle she occupied. He'd look like a gorilla riding behind a jaguar, he decided, but when the next bottle landed beside his boot, he made the move.

"I forgot my helmet," she said. Then turned the key. The engine grumbled. "Hold on."

He did, wrapping his arms around her waist and flattening himself over her back like a large bulky coat. She revved the engine and set them in motion, leaving a cloud of smoke and considerable rubber on the pavement.

He finally found the tiny footrests and decided this bike was designed for one person. A glance behind them showed an angry mob in the street.

He felt a pang of separation over leaving his sheriff's vehicle and worry over his SUV's welfare.

"Where are we going?"

"Kowa Nation," she called.

"Bad idea," he said. "They'll take your bike."

"I have to speak to their leadership."

He had to shout to be heard over the wind.

"Then let me call them. Pull over."

"Anyone following?" she asked, glancing in a side mirror.

"No. Pull in up there."

She did as directed, turning into the empty lot of the ice-cream stand now shut up tight for the evening. Drawing up beside one of the picnic tables, she rolled to a stop and braced her feet on either side, steadying the bike as he dismounted.

"That gang of thugs is selling weed in your county," she said.

"How do you know?"

She shook her head. "Can't say."

"Great. Thanks for the useless intel."

"You could use it and shut them down."

"I'm working on that and thanks again for telling me my job. But you see, I must catch them at it and have real evidence. That's how we do it up here."

She made a face and knocked down the kickstand, easing the sled to rest.

"Why didn't you draw your service weapon?" she asked.

He didn't answer but pressed gingerly at the lump emerging on his forehead with two fingers.

"The guy threw a punch. He didn't draw a weapon."

"He attacked a law enforcement officer."

"Just a way of reestablishing his personal space."

"You do know how to use a handgun?"

He blew away a breath through his nose and his teeth stayed firmly locked. His chin inclined just enough to give an affirmative answer.

"Guns, drawing them, shooting them, killing things. It doesn't solve problems. It only makes different ones."

She wondered about that answer. It seemed to come from some personal experience, and she thought of his army service record. Two confirmed kills, she recalled, the line of his personnel records coming back to her in a flash of perfect clarity.

"When was the last time you fired your pistol?"

"Hanau, Germany, 2008."

"You haven't drawn your sidearm in a decade?"

"Not a requirement of my position."

"Was this after you killed two servicemen in Germany?" she said, quoting from his records.

His eyes narrowed, glittering dangerously. "Yes."

"Will you tell me about that?"

"No. But you can read all about it on Google. May 1, 2008, one month before discharge, Hanau, Germany."

"But you would draw your weapon if circumstances demanded it."

"What circumstances?"

"To defend the citizens under your protection?"

"Yes."

"To protect yourself?"

"I don't think so."

She watched him swallow down something that seemed bitter, judging from his expression.

"Was it so terrible?"

"Taking another man's life? It's a scar on your soul."

"Then why pursue law enforcement?"

"More like it pursued me. Sheriff Rogers, the man I replaced at his retirement and for whom I have great respect, asked me to run for sheriff. He said I needed to get back in the saddle and that the county needed me."

"Seems you aren't really back."

"Most lawmen never have to draw their weapon."

That was true. And she really could not judge, because she had never been placed in the kind of situation he had faced.

"But you're not most people."

Axel gave her a long look and she felt, somehow, that he was taking her measure. He used the palms of his hands to scrub his cheeks as if trying to remove some invisible film. When he lifted his gaze to meet hers, he nodded, as if to himself.

"The report said two servicemen were involved in a drunken brawl. That the first serviceman drew his weapon on military police and that I ordered him to put down his weapon. He didn't. Instead, he drew on me and I shot him. Two shots and down he went. His partner charged me and I shot him, as well."

That was exactly what she had read.

Rylee pictured the bar in Germany, the drunken servicemen. The MPs called to restore order. She covered her hand with her mouth and then forced it down. She had asked and the least she could do was listen to him without sending judgment.

"But then there's the part that they don't put in the reports. There is the part that you see at night when you close your eyes. That first serviceman? He was drunk. Really, really drunk, according to his blood alcohol. When I shot him, he fell backward against the bar. He looked at me, and it was as if he suddenly realized what was happening. He seemed to me like a man who had just woken from some kind of a nightmare and into another one, where he had attacked an MP and now he was going to die. He knew it. He started to cry. His partner didn't have the opportunity…" His words trailed off. "He just…" Axel swallowed hard.

Rylee placed her hand on his. He turned his hand palm up and wove their fingers together, squeezing hard. Then he tried again.

"He just died instantly. I found out later, he was a newlywed expecting his first child. He was a boy. They named him after his father." Axel lifted his gaze and held hers. "That's the part they don't put in reports."

Rylee found her voice trembling when she spoke. "But you know that wasn't your fault. You were doing a job, responding to drunk and disorderly. That serviceman raised his weapon. Drew his weapon on you."

"His partner did what any good wingman would do, backed up his friend and it cost him his life."

"He attacked you."

"The price was too high."

"You had a right to defend yourself."

"There are other ways, Rylee. I could have thrown an empty bottle at him. Especially the second guy. He was drunk and he didn't have a weapon."

"He *was* a weapon, trained by the US Army."

"I think, believe, that a gun isn't the only option."

"It's the safest one."

"Safest?" He gave a mirthless laugh. "Not for the person on the wrong end."

He stared at her with eyes that beseeched her to understand. But she couldn't. Not really. Because she'd never faced such a situation. All she knew was that she was in no position to judge his feelings and that killing those two men had taken a toll on him. The urge to comfort overwhelmed. She stared up into those blue eyes and lost her way. Like a pilot flying in the infinite sky, there was nothing to help her recover her bearings.

She stepped forward, taking their clasped hands and bringing them behind her as she used the other to stroke the back of his neck, threading her fingers into his short thick hair. Rylee stepped closer, pressing her body to his.

He lowered his chin as his arms came around her. Rylee pressed her lips to his. Her urge to comfort dropped with her stomach as her body's reaction to his overwhelmed her. She reveled in the pleasure of his hungry kisses, as his strong hands stroked in a steady rhythm up and down her back. His mouth was velvet. She pressed herself to the solid wall of muscle as his arms enfolded her, taking her mouth with greater urgency.

Looking back on that first kiss, she would have liked

to take credit for drawing back first. As an analyst, she should have done some figuring and recognized that kissing the sheriff was a bad idea. But it was Trace that eased her away. He groaned as he broke the kiss, as if it cost him something to do so.

The next thing she knew, she was blinking up at him, missing the comforting heat of his body and the new buzz of desire that made her inch closer. He allowed it but simply knotted his hands behind her back and leaned away.

"What are you doing to me, Rylee?" he whispered. His voice was a soft rumble that seemed to vibrate low and deep inside her.

"Making a mistake." She followed that with a half smile.

"No doubt. And it's the sort of mistake that I might just approve of, but you said something about wanting to go to Kowa land?"

Her brain snapped back into action. How could she have forgotten the information she had been given by Agent Diel?

"They have something. That duffel. I need to get it back."

been kicked down a set of stairs, as the second drawer was too badly bent to close. Jeffries unlocked the filing cabinet with a small key and removed the duffel bag from the bottom drawer. Rylee's entire posture changed. She was on full alert with one hand on her weapon. Axel gave her a nudge and shake of his head. Her hand dropped back to her side.

Executive Council Member Jeffries set the duffel on the desk.

"We confiscated this from the person you pursued here," he said to Rylee. "We let them go. It seems to us that the carrier was Japanese. But I really don't know."

"Could he have been Chinese?" asked Rylee.

"I don't know." Jeffries rubbed the back of his neck. "It's possible."

"Has anyone looked inside this bag?"

Jeffries nodded. "Yes. Executive council and the acting chief of police have all seen the contents of this bag. We are in agreement that we do not want it on our lands but were not in agreement as to what to do with it."

Axel thought of the possibilities. What were the choices?

"Half the council was in favor of destroying it. The other half wanted to deliver it to state officials."

"Has anything been removed from this bag?" she asked.

"No."

She motioned to the bag. "May I?"

Jeffries nodded, extending a hand as he moved away.

"Why now?" asked Axel. "You could have given it to her when she first arrived."

"She didn't arrive. She entered our land without invitation. This negated any option to deal with her. Now she comes with a friend and with the escort of the sister of the chief of police."

Rylee flushed. "I am sorry for my bad manners. If I could, I would have done things differently."

Jeffries nodded. "Do them differently in the future. This is our home. How would you have reacted, if situations were reversed?"

"I would have deemed you a threat. I might not have been as forgiving as you have been."

Rylee turned her attention to the duffel. The way she unzipped the canvas bag gave Axel the chills. She moved as if the entire thing might explode.

"Is it volatile?" he asked.

"No. But if it is what I think it is, the contents are very dangerous."

"In what way?"

"I can't say," she said through clenched teeth, gingerly drawing back the sides of the bag.

Axel glanced in to see a second container of vinyl, rolled with a Velcro fastener. It reminded him of the sort of thing he used to carry lures for fly-fishing, only his version was canvas. Rylee lifted the orange-and-black bag to the desk and released the fastenings. Then she unrolled the container until it lay flat on the desk. The rectangular vinyl was divided into dozens of slots, each containing a glass vial.

"Ampoule transport roll," she said. Her voice had an airy quality and her breathing now came in short, rapid blasts from her nose.

"Get it out of here," said Jefferies.

"The foreign national carried this onto your land?" asked Rylee.

"No. This little guy crossed onto our land and we were in pursuit when we saw the drone with the duffel. Both in the same area, near the river. One of our people shot at the drone and it dropped the duffel, but we lost the thing in the trees near the river. Runner also got away. Recovered the package, though."

"A miracle it didn't break on impact," said Axel."

"Fell through the pine trees. My son caught it. And the guy who was there to retrieve it took off." Jeffries looked grim. "That spy came onto our land to retrieve this," Jeffries motioned at the bag, but now stood well back from the desk.

"Your son is very lucky. It was a good catch," said Axel.

"I was thinking the same thing."

Rylee rolled up the transport container holding the vials and then pointed at the duffel. "Burn that."

The rolled container went inside her leather jacket. She extended her hand to Jeffries and thanked him again. Then she turned and headed out of the storage building like a woman on a mission.

She had been correct, he realized. She had gone against the odds and gotten it right. But her people were all in the wrong place.

Axel thanked Jeffries and then jogged after Rylee.

Chapter Ten

The ride to Kinsley was a blur.

They stopped at her motel to switch from the motorcycle to her vehicle and collect the drone given to her by Stanley Coopersmith. Then they headed to his office in Kinsley.

As Rylee pulled to a stop at the curb, he saw his battered SUV parked before the station. Pete, of Pete's Garage, had beaten them here, managing to tow his sheriff's vehicle back. Axel paused on the sidewalk to take in the damage. One side looked as if it had slid a hundred yards on gravel. The sheriff's insignia had all but disappeared, along with most of the paint on the passenger side.

Rylee was like a schoolgirl, nearly skipping the distance between her car and his office. He unlocked the door and held it for her, then flicked on the lights.

Her expression was animated; she seemed to have an external glow, like a halo or aura surrounding her. In his office, she paced as she spoke with an excited ring to her voice. She kept the phone pressed to one ear and her finger in the other.

Rylee seemed to have completely forgotten he was

even there, as he took his seat and scrolled through his emails. Why did he care if she knew he was there or not? But he kept glancing her way, hoping to catch her eye. He didn't.

She described the cargo they had recovered. Arrangements were made for a pickup. After the call, she came to rest, collapsing into the big chair beside his battered wooden desk. The chair had been in the former sheriff's home, but when the stuffing began to show in one worn armrest, Rogers's wife had insisted it be banished from the house and it ended up here.

"Can you believe it?" She pressed one palm to her forehead and stared at the tiles of the drop ceiling above his desk. "I wish I could call my dad."

"It's not that late."

"He's in Guam again, I think. But, boy, I'd love to call him. I can't, of course. This isn't public info, but..." She smiled and sighed, happy in the prospect of telling her family of her coup.

"You were right." He moved to sit on the edge of his desk, keeping one foot planted on the floor. It didn't help. Rylee at close range still made him feel slightly motion sick. Did she know how pretty she was? "You gotta be pleased."

"More than pleased. Did I tell you that I'm one of seven? Seven!"

"No, you didn't tell me that."

"Oh, yeah. And as the youngest, I have never successfully commandeered my dad's attention for more than a minute at a time."

"Well, this ought to do it." He had lost his need to gain his father's respect the day he had asked his father which of the women in the compound his mother was and been told that it didn't matter.

Not to his father, maybe, but it sure did matter to Axel.

"What's he do, your dad?" *Besides ignore his daughter*, he wondered. Had he ever been that in need of his father's approval? He hoped not, but he admitted to himself that he had been back before he started sneaking off the compound. Only then did he begin to realize how twisted and aberrant his childhood really was. Early on he began to suspect that the warnings about the outsiders being damned had been a lie. A way to keep them all apart from anything that might undermine his father's control over them all. At first, he had sneaked off for attention. But no one had seemed to notice or care. If he hadn't left, would he right now be dressed in brown robes with his head shaved?

"My dad is a colonel in the US Marines, Indo-Pacific Command. All my brothers and my only sister are marines, too. I'm the black sheep, did not follow my marching orders."

"He wanted you to enlist?"

"Of course. He wanted me to attend officer training school and be a marine. He expected all of his children to serve their country."

"You are serving your country, Rylee. Working with Homeland Security would certainly fit that bill. He must know that," said Axel.

"Not according to my dad. You're either in the US Marines or you are not. There is no other option."

"So, your career choice caused some tension?" asked Axel.

"Oh, yeah," said Rylee. "I just didn't want to live my whole life out of the gunnysack. I wanted...wanted to find a place, one place to call home. Mom said home isn't a place. But you know, it could be."

"Except for my time in the service, I've lived my entire life in this county."

"Meanwhile, I didn't even know that there were families who did that. I saw from your records that you were emancipated. Is your family still here?" asked Rylee.

Why had he mentioned his past? Of course, she would have questions, but that did not mean he was ready or able to answer them. How did you even begin to explain the complicated mess that was his family? Let's just start with his mother. No, that was a terrible place to start. His father? Even worse.

"Just my dad. He's still around. I don't see him often."

Rylee's eager expression fell. She glanced away. "Oh, I see."

She didn't, though. How could she?

Axel forced a tight smile and she glanced away.

"I'm sorry about your mother."

He realized then that his words had led her to believe wrongly that his mom was dead.

Of course, Rylee was sorry for what she saw as a loss but she might be sorrier if she knew that his mother lived not ten miles from him and was not permitted to speak to her son or acknowledge him in any way as she prepared to enter Heaven's Door, as they called it. She had chosen his father's religious dogma over a relationship with him. That kind of rejection caused a sorrow that just never went away.

This would be the time to correct her and explain the situation. Axel groaned inwardly. His stomach knotted, and he knew he would not be doing that. Not today, not ever. Many of the good citizens of the county had forgotten that he was the skinny boy brought out of the Congregation of Eternal Wisdom by social services. They had forgotten that Sheriff Kurt Rogers had removed him from the influence of his father and fostered him for five years before Axel had joined the army.

His father had told Axel to his face that if he did not want to follow the true path to Heaven's Door, he could suffer the Desolation with the rest of the unbelievers. Axel's ears still burned at the memory of his father's scalding condemnation.

"Any brothers or sisters?" asked Rylee.

That was another complicated subject. One that he didn't even know how to begin to answer. Surely, he had brothers and sisters. But which ones were his by blood, who could say? The only way to sort that would be DNA testing and that would never happen.

Axel opted to keep his answer vague and truthful and then change the subject. "Yes. But you… Seven, right?"

"Exactly. I have five older brothers and an older sister, all in the marines."

Uh-oh, he thought. Each one would be glad to knock him in the teeth for what he wanted to do with their baby sister.

Rylee continued, "Oliver, the oldest, is a master sergeant in the Marine Air-Ground Force. Paul is a sergeant major in personnel. It burns Oliver up that Paul has a higher rank. Paul is stationed stateside in California. I have two twin brothers, Joshua and Grant.

They're both second lieutenants and both intelligence warrant officers in Hawaii. That's a great posting. Those two have done everything together since as far back as I can remember. Marcus is only two years older than me and an assault vehicles commander. Can you believe my only sister, Stephanie, is a gunnery sergeant in communications? She's working as a cyber-network operator in Germany."

"Your mom?"

"Mom worked in the military schools. She taught music. And I play guitar and strings because of her. But she passed five years ago of a lung infection."

"I'm sorry."

"Yeah." She took Axel's hand. "We have that in common—losing our mothers. Don't we?"

They didn't. He frowned.

"I know. It's hard, right? I think Josh and Grant were glad to reenlist, with her gone. Home isn't a home without a mom. Or at least that's how it was for us. We lived all over. Oceanside, Honolulu, Okinawa and then back to Hawaii, but Kāneʻohe Bay this time. We were in Jacksonville, which I liked, and then Beaufort, South Carolina, which I hated. But I was thirteen. Thirteen-year-olds hate most new things, I think, and moving. I detested moving. Maybe I just hate South Carolina because that's where she died. So, Dad got transferred from Guam to Germany. That way me and Stephanie and Marcus could be with him. My older brothers were all up and out, enlisted by then." She straightened as if someone had put an ice cube down her back. "Sorry, I didn't mean to unload all that baggage."

"It's all right. You know, families can be complicated." He set his teeth and looked at her open expression. Maybe Rylee could understand. She knew grief and separation and a dad who was emotionally unreachable. Only difference was she was still trying to reach hers. "Listen, about my father—"

Her phone chimed, and she darted to her feet, removing the mobile and staring at the screen.

"My boss," she said and took the call.

Thirteen minutes later there was a helicopter parked on centerfield of the community baseball field. Rylee jogged out, keeping low. He didn't know what he had expected but it was not to see Rylee, carrying both drone and samples, climb aboard and disappear behind the door. Before he could take a step in her direction, the chopper lifted off, sending the dirt on the infield swirling behind them.

"Didn't even say goodbye," he said, as he covered his face from the assault of rock and sand.

What was he thinking? That she was staying? This was a good reminder that she was on to bigger and better things. He told himself it was for the best. Best that she left before she discovered just where he had come from. Because if she stayed, sooner or later, she'd learn the truth and that was something that he just could not bear.

It was Thursday afternoon. After a long night and a few hours of sleep, Rylee was back in her office in Glens Falls. Somehow, everything seemed different, as if she didn't belong here.

Rylee held her cell phone in her palm, staring down at the contacts list. She had scored major points, located the vanguard of the attack and was just aching to crow about her accomplishment.

Her brow wrinkled as she realized that it was Axel she wanted to call. Not her father, who would likely be unavailable. He'd been unavailable emotionally to her for most of her life. Expecting him to suddenly see her as a competent protector of their country was just irrational. So why had she done all this?

If not for praise and advancement and accolades, why? Confusion rattled inside her like a bag of bolts in a barrel.

She hardly knew Axel. So why was she missing him and wanting to tell him everything that had happened since leaving him last night?

He was a bad choice for many reasons, not the least of which was the way he played fast and loose when deciding which laws to enforce.

For just a moment, she allowed herself to imagine an alternate reality. One where she came home to Axel every night. One where she stayed in one place and made a home for them. A garden with tomatoes and a bird feeder. Neighbors whose names you bothered to learn.

Rylee had spent her life moving and, while she'd believed she wanted something different, every decision she'd made climbing up the ranks had involved a move, and there was no end in sight. A promotion, the one she wanted so badly to earn, would require packing again and a new office, new city, new coworkers. Why had she never realized that in choosing to do the opposite, and not joining the US military, she had nevertheless adopted a transient lifestyle?

She sat hard as the realization hit her. She wasn't ever going to stop moving. She wasn't going to be a team player. Or be a welcome part of a group task force on anything. She was going to live a rootless existence, moving from one apartment to another with whatever she could carry in three suitcases. Just like her father.

She was never going to have that dog or those kids or that husband that she had believed she wanted. Was she?

Rylee scrolled through the contacts, past her family's names and her friends and her professional contacts, stopping on Axel Trace. Was she really going to pick him?

Suddenly, Rylee's accomplishment frightened her. It was what she wanted. To make a splash. To gain attention. To use her analysis skills and new field experience to move onward and upward.

So why was she thinking of a cool autumn night and a picnic table outside an ice-cream stand in the far reaches of New York State and the man who waited there?

Chapter Eleven

The knock upon Axel's door brought him grudgingly to his feet. Friday nights were busy, and he'd just made it home before eleven o'clock. The hour meant this was not a visitor. Most bad news came lately by phone or text, but some folks, the older ones mostly, stopped by to drop trouble on his door. Usually not after nine in the evening.

He had discovered that the later the hour, the larger the problem. Domestic, he decided as he left the kitchen in the back of the house, thinking the visitor would be a woman carrying her children in her arms, seeking protection. He'd stopped counting the number of such visits he'd taken since being elected as county sheriff.

Axel hiked up his well-worn sweatpants and grabbed a white T-shirt from the peg behind the door on his way past. He had changed for bed after his supper, but he'd cover up before he greeted his visitor. He had the shirt overhead when the knock came again.

He glanced through the window set high on the door and his breath caught. Rylee Hockings stood on his step dressed in a gray woolen jacket, thigh-hugging jeans and scuffed hiking boots. She was looking down at the yellow mums on his steps that had already been nipped by frost. The blossoms drooped and wilted. The angle of her jaw and the overhead light made her skin glow pink. The black knit cap on her head trapped her blond hair beside the slim column of her throat.

His breath caught, and his blood coursed, heated by her nearness. When was the last time a woman took his breath away?

Never was the answer. He'd steered clear of most women, recognizing the trouble they inherently caused and not wanting the complication of explaining the soul-scarring mess that was his family. Why would any woman, especially one as dedicated, smart and pretty as this one, want a man who most resembled the tangled wreckage of a submerged log in the river. He was good for tearing the bottom out of boats and causing other people trouble. So far, his personal life had been nothing but bad.

She lifted her fist, knuckles up, to knock again and glanced up to see him peering down at her.

"Hey! You gonna let me in?" she said, her voice raised to carry through the locked door that separated them.

He shouldn't. Because if he did, he had a fair idea where the evening might lead. She was smiling like a woman satisfied with the world, but he had the feeling he could change that smile, brighten it, perhaps remove the lines of tension bracketing those pink lips.

Axel turned the dead bolt, pulled open the door and stepped back.

"What a nice surprise."

She'd left Wednesday night and there had been no

d then mopped. Children assigned tasks on a
asis that grew increasingly difficult as they

een approaching that age where he would
expected to choose the most holy position
at the compound or the lesser status of men
ot accept the full preparation to be received
.
"

attention to her and realized he was

on all that's happe

"Sure." He thought the surprise must have
his face. Thus far, she had briefed him on ve

She breezed inside with the cool air, and
the door behind her. She stepped into the r
and sank to the bench with his shoes lined u
and the variety of coats hanging above on pe
that, the cubbies held his hats, gloves and a sof

"Boots off?" she asked.

He was happy to have her remove any iten
ing she wanted.

"Sure. And let m

calls, no texts and no emails from her or from Homeland Security. He'd decided that she'd dumped him like an empty beer bottle, and now he didn't know what to think.

"We've assembled a team. They'll be here tomorrow morning. I just wanted to brief you before their arrival on all that's happened."

"Sure." He thought the surprise must have shown on his face. Thus far, she had briefed him on very little.

She breezed inside with the cool air, and he closed the door behind her. She stepped into the neat entry and sank to the bench with his shoes lined up beneath and the variety of coats hanging above on pegs. Above that, the cubbies held his hats, gloves and a softball mitt.

"Boots off?" she asked.

He was happy to have her remove any item of clothing she wanted.

"Sure. And let me take your coat."

He waited as she worked loose the laces while also glancing into the living room. She slipped out of her boots, revealing new woolen gray socks. She was getting the hang of dressing for the weather up here, he thought. But Rylee was quick and used to adjusting to her environment. She must be, after so many moves.

She stood and he took her coat, using the opportunity to lean in to smell the fresh citrus scent at her neck before stepping back. Rylee headed to the living room. He had left it earlier, as he always did, pillows in line on the couch he used only for napping and his book waiting on the table beside his comfortable chair beside the remote.

"You're neat," she said, coming to a stop.

Having things, personal things, was something he never took for granted. Personal property was forbidden at the congregation. He could never have imagined owning a home of his own. Filling it with the over-stuffed comforts that were lacking in the austere landscape where he had been raised.

Wooden chairs placed on pegs each night. Floors swept and then mopped. Children assigned tasks on a weekly basis that grew increasingly difficult as they aged.

He'd been approaching that age where he would have been expected to choose the most holy position for males at the compound or the lesser status of men who did not accept the full preparation to be received in Heaven.

"Axel?"

He snapped his attention to her and realized he was clenching her coat in his fist.

"I asked if that was coffee that I smelled?"

The smile was forced but she didn't seem to notice. "Yes. Have you had supper yet?"

"Oh, hours ago, but I'd love a cup of coffee."

He debated where to bring her—the living room with that big couch or the dining room with the large wooden table for a professional conversation?

He motioned to the living room. "Make yourself comfortable. I'll bring you a cup. How do you take it?"

"Black."

He nodded and waited as she slipped into his world in her stocking feet. He was quick in the kitchen, returning with two cups. He tried not to place too much meaning on the fact that she sat on the sofa.

"Do you use the fireplace often?" she asked, gazing at the wood fireplace, screened and flanked with fire tools and a metal crate of kindling. The logs fit in an opening built in the river stone masonry for that purpose. The stone swept up to the twelve-foot ceilings of the old farmhouse and was broken only by the wide mantel crafted with chisels by hands long gone from the living, out of American chestnut back in a time when the tree was a plentiful hardwood.

"Yes, and I keep it set. Would you like a fire?"

"Oh, that's not necessary. It's just I always wanted a house with a fireplace. They don't usually have them in California or Hawaii—or Japan, for that matter."

"Or in South Carolina?"

She laughed, but her eyes were now sad. "That's right. How long have you been here?"

"Let's see, I found this place after I left the service. I bought the home after I finished my probation period with the City of Kinsley."

"Police Department," she said, quoting the part of his history that she obviously knew, the part that was in the records. But Sheriff Rogers had held back enough. Keeping the circumstances of his claim for emancipation listed as abandonment. The truth was worse and more complicated.

"That's right. So that was, wow, six years ago. And I still haven't replaced that back deck."

He set down her coffee and took a seat beside her. She gathered up the mug and took a sip.

"Strong," she said and set the ceramic back on the slate-topped coffee table.

He left her to set the fire. The entire process involved

striking a match and lighting the wadded newspaper beneath the tepee of kindling.

He slipped two logs from the collection and waited for the flames to lick along the kindling, catching the splinters in bright bursts of light.

"That's a pretty sight. Warms me up inside and out," said Rylee, gazing first at the fire and then to him.

An internal spark flared inside him and his heart rate thudded heavy and strong.

He knelt beside the fire and glanced back at her, taking in the relaxed smile and the warm glow of the firelight reflected from her cheeks and forehead. The entire world seemed to have taken on a rosy glow and he wasn't at all certain it was the fire's doing.

"Is it too late for a conversation?" she asked.

Did she mean too late in the evening or too late in their relationship? He'd spent the first few days resenting her intrusion, followed by a pervasive annoyance at the extra work she caused him. But just before she left, when they took that wild ride on the motorcycle, and even before that kiss, he knew there was something different about this woman. Perhaps the threat she posed was not professional but strictly personal.

Was that better or worse?

"No, it's not too late."

"Trace, I think I made a mistake with you. I want to apologize for trying to run you. You don't work for me and it was wrong for me to treat you as if you did. To come in here and tell you what to do in your own county. That's not collaboration. It's my first field assignment and I really want to do well. It's important for my career for me to get this experience. But even more important was finding the package. Finding that case will save a lot of lives."

He came to sit beside her on the sofa. "That's a good thing. But you're back, so I have to assume your work isn't finished." He didn't let himself latch on to the possibility that she'd come back to finish their business. "Do you want to tell me what this is all about?"

He waited in the silence that followed as she laced her fingers together and leaned forward until her forearms rested on her knees. Then she stared at the fire as it caught. He had time to add both logs to the blaze and return to his seat before she spoke.

"Yes, I think you deserve that. There was some trouble this summer—July—in the Adirondacks just south of here and in the city of Saratoga Springs." Her brows went up and she looked to him.

He nodded. "I know the area." He'd even gambled at the thoroughbred track a time or two in August.

"There was a CIA operative there. Apparently, he was collecting intel from a foreign agent on US soil, which breaks about fifty rules that I can think of. Regardless, the meet was made at Fort Ticonderoga and he retrieved a thumb drive full of intelligence. However, they were followed and our man had a difficult time getting the information into the hands of federal operatives. There was a civilian involved. A completely untrained, inexperienced woman, and how she survived I do not know. In any case, the intel leads them to believe there was a small sample of a biohazard, which they recovered. That told us what we were looking for. Unfortunately, the actual sample and the helicopter carrying it were shot down. This material went missing for part of

August. Apparently, it was discovered in a downed helicopter by an adventure specialist and a New York City homicide detective, who somehow managed to evade pursuit by foreign agents and successfully brought the intelligence to a state police office outside of Saratoga Springs, New York. The sample went to the CDC in Virginia."

The Centers for Disease Control, he knew, took care of all sorts of things, but as the name implied, they all had to do with diseases.

"Is it a pandemic?"

Chapter Twelve

Rylee's head dropped, and she gave a tired nod. "Yes, a pandemic."

Axel suddenly found it hard to breathe as visions of men and women in yellow hazmat suits cropped up in his mind like goldenrod.

"It's really bad," said Rylee. "What we collected were the samples to be used as prototypes for mass production."

His throat went tight and his breath caught as he remembered the yellow taped vials and the ones capped with red. "We also recovered an active vaccine."

"Vaccine?" asked Axel. That didn't sound too bad.

"The sample is a chemical weapon we have been tracking for months. It's a deadly strain of the flu."

"If it is a weapon," asked Axel, "why bring a vaccine?"

"They would want their people vaccinated before releasing the virus," said Rylee.

"How will it be released?" asked Axel, bracing his hands on his knees as he awaited the answer.

"We don't know," said Rylee. "A subway at rush hour. An outdoor concert. A Renaissance festival. The beach. Anywhere, really, where there is a crowd. It's airborne and does not die on surfaces. Technically, they could dust it on anything—the railing of a cruise ship, the escalator at a mall, a single suitcase on a baggage carousel at Dulles Airport."

A chill went up his back as tiny needles of dread seemed to pierce his skin.

"This is not the average seasonal flu," said Rylee. "It's a whole different animal. A pandemic. Virulent. They compared a possible outbreak to something like the influenza epidemic of 1918, which killed more people than World War I. And it attacked people ages twenty to forty. Not the old or the very young, but healthy adults. It killed fifty million people with a mortality rate of 2.5 percent. The CDC estimates that this strain has a mortality rate of 12.4 percent in unvaccinated populations."

Axel felt sick to his stomach. Why hadn't he helped her from the start?

"My office has been running different scenarios and possible targets. The intelligence that we received indicates that this virus will be used in a biological attack. Prior to the attack, the intelligence collected indicates that the active virus strains would be delivered across the border. We have been on high alert, trying to discover where the crossing would be made."

"And you thought the crossing would be here on my border. And your supervisors thought Buffalo."

"Yes, that's right. We weren't sure if the biological agent would be coming across in a large container or if the terrorists were planning to incubate the virus here within our borders. We now have our answer. They're going to manufacture here."

Axel placed a hand on her knee. "But you found it. You got the virus before they could turn it over to the manufacturing plant."

"Well, that's partly true. We did get it. But we can say, with fair confidence, that they will try again. This size of a load makes it easy to carry and hard to find. The load will likely not be carried in a tractor trailer, train car or ocean liner, as we theorized. That's why we're deploying here. We think they'll use similar tactics. If they get through, if they put this virus into production, lives will be lost. It would be bad, Axel. Really, really bad."

He sat back in the couch, drew his hands together and wrapped them around his body. His quiet little county had become ground zero.

He thought that he knew this place so well. Now he wondered if he ever knew it at all. His home had become the front line in a war on terror. The truth horrified him. He thought of that virus coming again into his country and getting loose and the lives that would be lost if they did not stop it.

"Who is behind this?" he asked.

"The CIA operative who had secured the intel called the group Siming's Army. Simings are creatures or deities, perhaps, from Chinese mythology. They are referred to as Masters of Fate, and Judges of Life, and as worms—The Three Worms, I believe. These deities are said to enter the body at birth. They are supposed to mark an individual's good and bad actions on earth and use that information to calculate a person's life span.

Each worm rules a different body system—mind, body, heart. When your time is up, one of the worms attacks."

"Well, that's terrifying."

"So is this group. Because we had never heard of them before, their motives are murky."

"What do they want?"

"We believe that they think that the US has committed evil on the earth and Siming's Army will exact revenge. Judge us for our actions. We hypothesize that they will attack our heart, mind and body, metaphorically."

"What's the heart?"

"We don't know. Our children. Our citizens. New York City. Congress. The Mall of America. We just don't know."

"The mind?"

"Electrical grid. Internet. The federal government. Again, open to debate."

"This pandemic is the attack of only one of the Masters of Fate. The one on our body?"

"That's right. We believe the virus is the attack meant for that system."

Meaning there were two others, heart and mind, still out there.

"What do we do now?" he asked.

"Go through our suspects again. Find who is helping the motorcycle gang with this cargo."

"You can cross off the Kowa," he said. "At least that's my belief based on their willingness to turn this over to us."

He glanced to her and she nodded. "I agree."

"So, who's on your short list?"

"We are fairly certain that the North Country Riders are involved with the transporting of either foreign nationals, the virus or possibly both. We don't think they're working alone because they don't have the compound or any sort of home base to secure the virus. Also, they have no banking system. Our people can't follow their money because they don't seem to handle any."

"They transport weed. I know they get paid," said Axel.

"Cash, it seems. So who are their bankers?" Rylee blew out a breath in a long audible sigh. "It's my supervisor's opinion that they would be working with someone like the Mondellos."

"The moonshiners?"

"Well, they have a home base and they're well protected. They are an established farm with trusts and way more money than they should have, though we have yet to track it all down. Their money operation was described to me as complicated and sophisticated."

"And they have border perimeter security and boats to cross the St. Lawrence into Canada," said Axel. "But to attack their own country?"

"They're high on our list."

"What about the survival group? Coopersmith has a compound, as well. And he's not only fortified but heavily armed. And they believe that the end of the world is coming. They'd survive a pandemic. I'm certain."

"Yes, they are also contenders. They might have given us the drone as a way of removing suspicion."

"So you are surveilling both groups?"

"Yes."

And he had been annoyed that he had had to pull her butt out of trouble both times. He should have been helping her. Should have known that there was a credible threat. She wouldn't be here, otherwise.

"I'm sorry, Rylee. I should've been more help. I should have trusted that you had good instincts and good information."

She twisted in her seat so that she was facing him. Her smile was sad and her eyes luminous. He thought of their kiss and wished he could kiss her again.

"Is this a fresh start?" she asked.

"I think so. I'd like it to be."

She reached out and took his hand. He stroked the back of hers with his thumb.

"And you're willing to work with me?" she asked.

"I'll do everything I can to help you."

"Wonderful. One of the groups we are now targeting is the Congregation of Eternal Wisdom. You're familiar?"

Despite the warmth of the room, a chill rolled up Axel's spine and into his chest until his heart iced over. He drew back, leaning against the armrest.

Was he familiar? He was. But he did not want to be the one to bring Rylee to them.

She went on. "They have nonprofit status and are not required to do an annual report. Every nonprofit exempt from income taxes, must file an annual return, except churches."

"What?"

"It's true. Fraud within churches is a major problem, as is mismanagement and money laundering. Very tough to prosecute with the separation of church and state. Most goes unreported. We believe that little of the money collected by this organization from members' estates, donations, retreats and sale of religious products is being used for the congregation's preservation. Numbers don't add up. That means they have established a banking system. They could be the bankers for whatever group is assisting Siming's Army."

"They could launder money collected by the ones paid to carry the load?"

"That's correct."

"That outfit is dangerous. They're especially dangerous to women. You should not be the one to go there. Send some of your men."

She cocked her head as if something now interested her. "You are the second one who's told me that this outfit is dangerous for women. The first was my colleague with DHS. What exactly is going on out there?"

Axel sat back and rested his head on the sofa. He stared up at the ceiling. He didn't remember when he started talking, but he did. He told her what he knew of the cult. He went on and on, but he left out one important detail. One piece of information that he knew would send her out of his house and break their new collaboration. He just did not have the courage to tell her that he'd been born and raised inside the order of the Congregation of Eternal Wisdom.

Chapter Thirteen

Rylee waited as Trace contemplated her question. She knew about the cult. She had even been out there to speak to their leader, Reverend Wayne. From what she could see, the residents there were of an extreme belief but did seem to be content and grounded. They lived communally and from a quick overview, she believed they had adopted some of the tenets from Buddhism, Taoism, and perhaps the old Shaker communities that use to thrive in upstate New York at the turn of the last century, until their tenet toward celibacy brought the group to the obvious end. In this community, both men and women were covered up. All seemed happy. And committed to preparing themselves for what they saw as the upcoming end of humanity's time on earth.

The reverend had left her to speak to the two social strata of men distinguishable by whether they grew facial hair. And to the women, who did not seem subjugated or threatened. She could see the children but had not spoken to them. Her observation was that they were on the thin side but there were no visible indications that they were not well cared for and developing normally.

"Is there something going on out there, Axel, that you want me to be aware of?" asked Rylee.

Trace scrubbed his hand over his mouth and then turned to face her. The fire had taken the chill from the air, leaving her with a pleasant lethargy brought on by a sudden pause in the frantic preparations and debriefing that had been the last two days.

"People up here give them a wide berth," he said. "We know that the folks who come from all over to join them are very committed to their beliefs that the end of the world is near. The reverend, however, seems more committed to being certain that the newest members of his flock are stripped of all personal possessions and assets upon joining. The reverend seizes these for the betterment of his congregation. I have been in contact with the IRS about this but, as he is a nonprofit and a church, investigating him is tricky. A cursory look came back with nothing suspicious."

"I can ask some friends at the Treasury to have another look," said Rylee. "But if they already came back with nothing… Why are you so certain something illicit is happening out there?"

"A feeling that I have. A bad feeling."

The silence settled over them like a warm blanket. She was growing comfortable with him. There was no pressure to fill the warm dry air with useless prattle. She watched a log roll in the flame, sending a shower of sparks below the grate. The embers glowed orange and gradually faded to gray. She loved the smell of wood smoke. Somehow, in her traveling from place to place, it had always been a comfort. Their home in Germany had had a fireplace and she used to beg her parents to light the fire. They did very occasionally, as her mother did not trust that the chimney had been correctly cleaned.

She caught him staring at her, seeing a different kind of fire in his eyes. The need he stirred in her had gained in strength. What at first had been an annoyance and a distraction, had gathered into an internal storm that was getting out of her control.

She glanced back to the flames. She had told him everything and that felt good. Instead of making her anxious, the information felt like what she should have offered at the start—a collaboration with local law enforcement. If she weren't so suspicious of everyone, she would have done this earlier.

He was a decorated officer with an exemplary military record. True, he had been in the US Army, but she wasn't going to hold that against him. She wasn't like her dad, seeing one branch of the military as superior to the rest. And he had come home and gotten his education, without the help of family to do that, applying for aid and to colleges. Getting that first job right here in Kinsley's police force and then being elected by the county at such a young age. Clearly, his community had faith in him. Unless those same citizens on his watch list had made sure that he was elected.

Her smile waned but she pushed back the doubts.

No, there was no evidence or even speculation to that effect. It was only her problems with trust that made her so reluctant to believe in him.

Trust. And that was the trouble. Or at least what the counselor at school had suggested to her. The free mental health service offered through the health and wellness center at her college. The mental health profes-

sional who had advised she come weekly and proposed
to her that her tendency to avoid relationships might be
due to her experience of losing any friends due to the
frequent moves. And that her difficulty forming an at-
tachment with a partner might be due to her father's
emotional distance and physical absence.

You don't trust men to stick around, she had said.

Yet, this man had stuck around in his county despite
having no family here. Parents listed as unknown on
official records. Sheriff Rogers's report listed him as
abandoned. Yet Axel said his dad was still around. Had
his father abandoned him or was he unable to care for
his child? It was also possible that his father had been
deemed unfit as a parent, but then there would be a
record. The entire thing was mysterious. In any case,
how complicated must his feelings for his father be?

That blank spot in his past troubled her. Where had
he been before his appearance in official reports? The
records yielded nothing. Where had he been for thirteen years?

"Would you like something other than coffee? I have
beer and white wine."

"You don't seem like a wine guy."

"Former girlfriend," he admitted.

Red flags popped up before her like traffic cones in
a construction area.

"Should have improved with age, because she left it
over two years ago."

"Anyone since?"

"No one serious. I'm not in a relationship, Rylee, if
that's what you're asking."

"I'm not." But of course, she was, and the reason she

cared if he were available made her ears buzz and her stomach ache with dread because it meant that she was considering one—a relationship—with Sheriff Axel Trace. *Not him*, she told herself.

"So, wine?"

"No, not her wine. I'll have a beer."

He chuckled and stood, removing the barely touched coffee and heading out. With both hands full, he could do nothing about the low-slung sweatpants and Rylee nearly fell off the couch staring at the dimples at his lower back and the tempting curve of his butt.

"You should get out of here right now," she muttered to herself. She folded her arms over her chest and sat back in the chair. Her gaze fixed on the fire, burning low and giving a soft crackle as the logs surrendered to the flames.

He returned with two beers in glasses. That earned points. He set hers beside her on the table and returned to his seat with his; only this time, he took the center cushion, closer to her. The proximity brought his scent to her.

Wood smoke, something stronger and new. Had he put on cologne while he was gone? Whatever it was, it was sexy as hell. She leaned to retrieve her new drink and took a long swallow. The bubbly brew cooled her throat. They sat quietly, with the outward semblance of calm. Only her heart was thumping like a rabbit caught in a snare, and his jaw clenched as he held a smile that seemed forced.

"This is such a nice room," she said. That brought a beautiful smile to his face, transforming his usual serious, dour demeanor into something breathtaking. A trickle of excitement moved inside her.

"I picked out everything." The pride was clear in his voice and with good reason. He had an eye for masculine homey touches.

Were they going to do this?

He caught her gaze and held it. He set aside her drink and then his own. Then he extended his hand, palm up, offering himself to her.

"I want to kiss you again," he said.

"Is that right?" she asked.

He nodded, his gaze never wavering from hers. A luscious tingle danced over her skin and her cheeks felt hot.

"It's a bad idea. Long-term, I mean," he said. "I'm staying. You're going. That doesn't give us a lot of time."

"Time is overrated," she said.

His smile broadened. And he gave a dry chuckle that warmed her inside and out.

"Is that a yes on the kissing?" he asked.

She grinned. "That's a yes."

She took his offered hand and he dragged her into his arms. She settled beside him, feet on the sofa and arms hooked around his neck.

"What if we do more than kissing?" he asked.

"I'm open to more."

She waited for him to kiss her, but instead he let his gaze roam over her face, down her neck and then return, retracing his course until his gaze fixed on her mouth. She drew her lips between her teeth and dragged her bottom lip free. She watched him swallow, his Adam's apple bobbing. The room no longer felt warm but hot.

The tension between them coiled like a spring. Still, she waited. She hoped he'd make the first move. Instead, he let his head drop back to the sofa and closed his eyes. Squeezed them tight as if the only way to resist her was to remove her from his sight. She took the opportunity to study his features. The thickness of his dark brow. The length of his feathery lashes. The slight flush that covered his cheeks and neck. The strong muscles that flanked the column of his throat. And the interesting wisp of dark hair that emerged from the top of the shirt. She had caught him dressed in little. She suspected he wore only a T-shirt and not a thing beneath the thin sweatpants. When she'd knocked, had he already been ready for bed? Would he consider taking her along?

Waiting was overrated, too, she thought. If he knew that she was not staying and that she knew he was not going, she did not see any reason why they should not spend the evening together. It was not a conflict of interest. They were no longer on opposite sides. He had agreed to help her with her investigation, and she had shared what information she had. They were both consenting adults.

The more she rationalized her decision, the more she had to push down the demons of doubt. Why was she trying so hard to convince herself that sleeping with Axel Trace would not be a mistake?

Somewhere in her heart, she recognized that starting something she could not finish with this man was dangerous. She should crawl off his sofa, find her boots and march herself out of his house. She should go back to the motel and continue reading through the mountain of paperwork associated with this investigation.

He released her with surprising strength, lifting her effortlessly off his lap and onto the seat beside him. Then he stood and stripped out of his shirt before stooping to strip off her socks. She stood then, and he unfastened her jeans, sliding them down her legs. Dressed in only a tiny scrap of white lace, Rylee waited.

"You're so beautiful," he said, his voice low as if they were in church.

"Back at you," she said and offered her hand. "Rug or couch?"

"Ladies' choice."

Rylee pointed to the sofa. Then stretched out on her back and beckoned to him. He came to her, offering her a small open packet, protecting her again. She rolled the condom over him. He squeezed his eyes shut as he sucked in a breath at her touch. She lay back and he came to her, barrier between them. His body burned. His hot, firm flesh pressed tight to her damp skin. She opened her legs and he glided into her. She savored the steady rhythm and the delicious friction. His spicy scent mingled with the smell of leather and wood smoke.

She wouldn't think about why this was the wrong man at the wrong time. Rylee arched back, closing off all doubts and warnings and, oh, yes... This was what she wanted. Him making love to her here, safely hidden away from the rest of the world and their judgments and rules.

She closed her eyes to savor the perfection of his being.

And as she moved with him, the rest of her thoughts faded until all she could do was catch the rising wave of pleasure that shattered her to pieces before dropping

But she couldn't. Some unnamable part of her could do nothing else.

She ignored reason and her better judgment. She ignored caution and fear. She ignored doubt, as she pressed herself against him and lowered her mouth to his.

Chapter Fourteen

Axel's grip about Rylee tightened as she deepened the kiss. Her insides began a persistent aching to touch his skin. The impulse to drag away every barrier that separated them built to a roar, drowning out the receding whisper of doubt.

This was right. This was perfect, and she wanted all of him. Rylee broke the kiss and felt his resistance in the tightening of his grip before he allowed her to lean back. His confused expression made her smile. She could see the rising beat of need tighten his jaw and burn in his hungry gaze.

She wasn't teasing him and it took only an instant to drag the long-sleeved shirt over her head, leaving her in nothing from the waist up except her white lace bra.

His mouth hung open for a moment and he made a sound in his throat, like a sigh, then he reached for her. Warm hands splayed across her bare back. The contact thrilled, and they shared a smile.

"You really want to do this, Rylee?" he asked.

"Seems so."

"I'm going to need you to give me a definitive answer here."

"Yes, Sheriff Trace, I want to make love to you, right here and now, in front of this lovely fire on this soft leather couch." She ran a finger down his forehead and nose, pausing on his lower lip. "Definitive enough?"

In answer, he took her index finger in his mouth and sucked. The smile fell from her lips as his tongue swirled about the sensitive pad of her finger. Her mind did the rest, anticipating the pleasure he had in store for her. Rylee's eyes fluttered closed and her head fell back. He released her finger as his hands moved to her torso and he leaned her forward, kissing the center of her chest, just below the collarbone. Then his tongue painted tiny swirls on her flesh.

Axel stroked her back as his mouth moved from the top of one breast to the next. She felt the clasp at the back of her bra release. Free from the constraints, she shrugged out of the lace and tossed it aside.

His hands reversed course, coming between the as she straddled his lap. He lifted her. The callous rough feel of his palms on her sensitive skin gave an erotic thrill matched only by the look of long on his face. His focus dropped from her face t breasts. She leaned in and he licked one nipp hard, aching bud.

This time she groaned. The need that ha her up now turned liquid and she gave in to move on top of him, rocking back and sucked one nipple and then the next, ta and making her crazy.

She tugged at his shirt, dragging it ders and then raking her nails over of his back.

But she couldn't. Some unnamable part of her could do nothing else.

She ignored reason and her better judgment. She ignored caution and fear. She ignored doubt, as she pressed herself against him and lowered her mouth to his.

Chapter Fourteen

Axel's grip about Rylee tightened as she deepened the kiss. Her insides began a persistent aching to touch his skin. The impulse to drag away every barrier that separated them built to a roar, drowning out the receding whisper of doubt.

This was right. This was perfect, and she wanted all of him. Rylee broke the kiss and felt his resistance in the tightening of his grip before he allowed her to lean back. His confused expression made her smile. She could see the rising beat of need tighten his jaw and burn in his hungry gaze.

She wasn't teasing him and it took only an instant to drag the long-sleeved shirt over her head, leaving her in nothing from the waist up except her white lace bra.

His mouth hung open for a moment and he made a sound in his throat, like a sigh, then he reached for her. Warm hands splayed across her bare back. The contact thrilled, and they shared a smile.

"You really want to do this, Rylee?" he asked.

"Seems so."

"I'm going to need you to give me a definitive answer here."

"Yes, Sheriff Trace, I want to make love to you, right here and now, in front of this lovely fire on this soft leather couch." She ran a finger down his forehead and nose, pausing on his lower lip. "Definitive enough?"

In answer, he took her index finger in his mouth and sucked. The smile fell from her lips as his tongue swirled about the sensitive pad of her finger. Her mind did the rest, anticipating the pleasure he had in store for her. Rylee's eyes fluttered closed and her head fell back. He released her finger as his hands moved to her torso and he leaned her forward, kissing the center of her chest, just below the collarbone. Then his tongue painted tiny swirls on her flesh.

Axel stroked her back as his mouth moved from the top of one breast to the next. She felt the clasp at the back of her bra release. Free from the constraints, she shrugged out of the lace and tossed it aside.

His hands reversed course, coming between them as she straddled his lap. He lifted her. The calloused, rough feel of his palms on her sensitive skin gave her an erotic thrill matched only by the look of longing on his face. His focus dropped from her face to her breasts. She leaned in and he licked one nipple to a hard, aching bud.

This time she groaned. The need that had burned her up now turned liquid and she gave in to the urge to move on top of him, rocking back and forth. Axel sucked one nipple and then the next, taking his time and making her crazy.

She tugged at his shirt, dragging it up to his shoulders and then raking her nails over the exposed skin of his back.

He released her with surprising strength, lifting her effortlessly off his lap and onto the seat beside him. Then he stood and stripped out of his shirt before stooping to strip off her socks. She stood then, and he unfastened her jeans, sliding them down her legs. Dressed in only a tiny scrap of white lace, Rylee waited.

"You're so beautiful," he said, his voice low as if they were in church.

"Back at you," she said and offered her hand. "Rug or couch?"

"Ladies' choice."

Rylee pointed to the sofa. Then stretched out on her back and beckoned to him. He came to her, offering her a small open packet, protecting her again. She rolled the condom over him. He squeezed his eyes shut as he sucked in a breath at her touch. She lay back and he came to her, barrier between them. His body burned. His hot, firm flesh pressed tight to her damp skin. She opened her legs and he glided into her. She savored the steady rhythm and the delicious friction. His spicy scent mingled with the smell of leather and wood smoke.

She wouldn't think about why this was the wrong man at the wrong time. Rylee arched back, closing off all doubts and warnings and, oh, yes… This was what she wanted. Him making love to her here, safely hidden away from the rest of the world and their judgments and rules.

She closed her eyes to savor the perfection of his loving.

And as she moved with him, the rest of her thoughts receded until all she could do was catch the rising wave of pleasure that shattered her to pieces before dropping her safely back between the soft folds of the sofa and the warmth of Axel's embrace.

She dozed. Rousing when his fingers danced up her shoulder as he kissed her neck, humming his pleasure.

They snuggled together on the wide leather sofa, the fire heating the room. Something about the feel of him, his scent and the strength of his big solid body made her feel grounded and at home. She stroked the warm velvet of his back, savoring the feel of his skin when his voice rumbled through his chest.

"Do you like it up here on the river?" he asked.

"It's got a rugged beauty," she said, hearing the languor in the slowness of her voice.

"Would you ever think of staying?"

The languor dissolved, and she stiffened. What was he asking?

"I've got plans, career plans to earn an assignment in New York City."

He made a disapproving sound. "You ever been there? It's noisy and dirty and crowded."

"And a major assignment."

"I thought you said you wanted to stop moving from place to place."

"Well, yes. But after I get promoted."

The rumble in his chest was back, sounding like a growl.

"No end to that. Just like your childhood being dragged from one posting to another. Only this time you are doing it to yourself. Don't you want a home, Rylee?"

She scowled. Her career advancement involved a willingness to travel. Getting to New York would put her in a place to make a real difference. She looked forward to telling her family, imagined the conversation with her father. It was important to do well, more important since she was not in the military.

She lifted to an elbow to look down at his handsome face, marred only by the frown tugging at his mouth.

"Would you ever consider leaving this county?"

His answer was immediate. "I can't."

"Because of your job. Elected official?"

"I know this place. Everything I am is because I was born in Onutake County. There are real good people here and then there's the ones that bear watching. I'm here for them, to be here when things go bad."

"You sound like it's a foregone conclusion."

"It is."

"Anyone specific?"

"The Congregation of Eternal Wisdom."

"Ah," she said. "We talked about them. They're on my watch list."

"They definitely should be."

"You have information on any illegal activities?"

"Just bilking vulnerable people out of their life's savings and twisting their beliefs to Reverend Wayne's version of faith."

"Not illegal, as I've said."

"Immoral, then."

"That's why you stay? Because of that religious order."

"It's a cult."

She swallowed back her disappointment. Was that a lump in her throat? What was happening to her?

She had enjoyed sleeping with him, but she wasn't

looking for a relationship. Who was she kidding? Sleeping with Axel had been mind-blowing and now that she could think again, she realized she was in real trouble.

"So, you're needed here." Why did she even want to know and why was she holding her breath?

"I am. Maybe someday I'll be free of this place."

AXEL WOKE IN the gray predawn light, lying on his back with Rylee beside him. She slept on her side, pressed between the leather back of the couch and his body. One arm lay on his chest, with her palm pressed flat over his heart. Her cheek rested on his shoulder and her mouth was open as she gave a soft snore with each intake of breath. Her top leg was coiled about one of his, so that her foot and ankle threaded beneath his opposite calf.

She'd asked him if he'd ever leave the county. Nothing had tempted him so much as her question. The tug to be with her was new, like some invisible cord drawing him to her.

Then there was his father and his promise to see Axel suffer for daring to leave the fold. He knew exactly how his father might do that; he could call his followers together and, at his word, they would all return to their rooms and take their lives. That included the children, his siblings, who had stayed and the mother he could not even name. She was there among the other women, one of them. He'd tried shutting them down and failed. He didn't have the authority. His father knew that and seemed to bask in Axel's powerlessness.

Rylee's skin was covered in gooseflesh. The fire had burned out and the air in the room held the chill

that told him the forecasted cold front had arrived. His
arm was under her and his fingers splayed over one
perfect orb of her ass. He resisted the urge to squeeze.
Instead, he lifted his opposite hand and dragged the
fleece blanket from the back of the chair, covering their
naked bodies. Rylee hummed her satisfaction and then
nestled closer.

One eye opened and she peered up at him.

"Hello, gorgeous," he whispered and brushed a
strand of blond hair from her cheek, tucking it behind
the shell of her ear.

"I've got to pee." She pushed up and groaned. "Freezing in here."

"Take the blanket," he said.

In a moment, he had the fleece around her shoulders.

"What about you?" she asked.

"Heading to my bed. Care to join me?"

"Sounds reasonable." She grinned and then went
down the hall toward the guest bathroom as he headed
to the master.

They reconvened in his king-size bed, where she
dropped the fleece in favor of the down comforter and
flannel sheets and him.

"Oh, the sheets are cold," she said, shivering.

"Not for long," he promised.

When they finally stopped warming the sheets and
each other, the bedding was tangled about his waist, two
of the pillows were somewhere on the floor and they
were both panting. He gathered her in, their moist skin
sticking them together like Post-its. He smiled, tucking
her head under his chin as he embraced her.

He had known they'd be good together, but Rylee in

the flesh was so much better than anything he could ever have imagined. She was bold and more uninhibited than he would have guessed. In her professional life, Rylee was exacting, demanding and a pain in his butt.

In his bed, she was generous, thrilling and the best thing to happen to him in forever. He wondered if she had an early start and if she didn't, if he could manage to keep up with her.

He grinned like a fool at the ceiling of the quiet room as Rylee's breathing changed. His entire body felt sated and relaxed, and he had the suspicion that it was not just having sex with an amazing woman that he had to thank. It was sleeping with Rylee. He really wanted to please her and to give her a piece of himself that he had kept from all the others. He wanted her to know him as no one else had. The smile began to fade.

Why was that?

He wasn't stupid enough to think that if he were good enough in bed, she might not want to leave him. Was he?

He pressed his free hand to his forehead and groaned. That was exactly what he thought. If they were perfect together, she might just change her mind about this case and her promotion and quit everything to live forever in his arms.

He was, in layman's terms, an idiot.

As if to prove his point, Rylee's phone alarm sounded from the living room and she was up and retrieving the device before he could even drag the pillow from his face. He opened his eyes to see the golden light of morning made richer from the reflection off the yellow leaves of the sugar maple that occupied much of the backyard. The next thing he saw was Rylee dressed in her wrinkled jeans and rumpled shirt, still barefoot as she crossed before the bed, staring at her phone. She disappeared into the bathroom without even glancing at him in the bed.

That was bad, he knew. Really bad. He'd made more than a few hasty exits after spending the night somewhere that, in the morning, seemed like a mistake.

He dropped back into the pillows. Morning had come, and he needed to play it cool as if this were just one of those things, except it wasn't. Maybe he should tell her that.

Or never tell her that. The sound of the water running brought him to his feet. Images of Rylee, soapy with suds rolling down her body, sent him to the bathroom door. His hand on the knob, he paused. Then he realized it was the water running into the sink and that a closed door was a clear indicator that she did not want his company.

His hand fell to his side.

"Breakfast?" he called.

"Sorry. I've got to run."

And what had he really thought she would do? Call her boss and resign?

Axel dragged himself back to bed and realized that his hamstrings were sore and that he was still naked. He needed to start running again.

"Run away from Rylee, maybe," he muttered. The chill in the air made him choose jeans and a flannel shirt, which he dragged on over a clean white T-shirt.

He headed to the kitchen, hoping that some fresh brewed coffee would wake him up to the fact that what had rocked his world had clearly not been an earth-moving experience to Rylee.

He didn't like being a workout dummy. Question was, should he tell her so or cross his fingers and hope she needed him again?

Chapter Fifteen

Rylee blinked at herself in the medicine cabinet mirror. Her hands were on the edge of his sink, only inches from his shaving cream, razor, toothpaste and toothbrush that lined the back of the countertop.

Had she lost her mind?

Obviously, she had lost her mind because the sex with the sheriff had been mind-blowing. Hard as it was to admit she had never experienced that sort of a connection with anyone in her past. Note that her past wasn't littered with hundreds of lovers, but she had had enough of them to know that what she and Axel had shared was unique, and that made her realize it was dangerous.

She wanted to get out of there as quickly as possible and find somewhere she could think. Somewhere where her view did not include the wide, tempting expanse of Axel's bare chest. She needed her brain and not her instincts to guide her.

Certainly, she knew better than to sleep with a coworker. Axel was not actually a coworker or a subordinate, but he was a local associate and that made this a bad idea. The sort of idea that could end a career. And here she was so close with a real breakthrough and solid evidence that this place had been used by the terrorists to smuggle some of the biohazard.

The troops were on their way. Her boss was on her way. She'd already received a text with Lieutenant Catherine Ohr's ETA. And she'd received them while naked in Axel's bed.

She wanted very much to be dressed in a clean, ironed suit when she met her superior, rather than the rumpled mess of clothing that had clearly been scooped up off the floor and hastily donned on her way out.

Coffee. She needed coffee, but she also needed to get out of here first. She did not want to have a conversation with Axel. She did not want to explain her reluctance to continue with something that was so devastatingly wonderful that she could not wait to see him again and wanted very much to crawl back under that giant fluffy coverlet and explore every inch of that amazing body. It was one thing to have a body that was as perfectly formed as Axel's and was quite another to know how to use it to the best effect. And he ticked every box. She was still ticking as a result. Her leg muscles ached with fatigue and yet, here she was trying to think of a way that she could see him without having any of her colleagues find out. No.

"Bad idea," Rylee said to her reflection, wagging a finger at herself for emphasis.

Rylee found his spray deodorant, pressed the button, sniffed and decided against it. What she needed was a shower. She didn't need to add more of Axel's scent to her skin. She glanced toward the shower and then shook her head. She paused only long enough to draw a long breath and close her eyes before emerging into his bedroom. He was, thankfully, fully dressed in his casual clothes and sitting on his unmade bed. White T-shirt, open blue flannel shirt and faded blue jeans. His feet were bare, and she found the sight of his long toes dusted with hair instantly arousing.

She groaned.

"You okay?" he asked.

"I'm not sure." She forced herself to stop fidgeting and stood still before him. "Axel, did we just make a mistake?"

His mouth went tight, and his brow descended. He glanced away from her and then back. Then he rose to stand before her, close enough to touch, but he did not reach out.

"I don't know, Rylee. Only time will answer that. I do know that I don't regret what happened between us. I'm sorry if you do."

Her hands were clasped, and she spun the titanium ring she had commandeered from her brother Paul that encircled her thumb as if it were a spinner. What to say?

"I'm not sure we have very much in common," she said, feeling it a bad start. Her belief was confirmed by the narrowing of his eyes.

"We have this in common," he said, motioning to his bed. The covers looked as if they had been twisted and tossed by the ocean and then cast ashore to dry. "And we have the fact that you cared enough about me last night to share my bed."

"My timing is bad. My supervisor is en route, and I only have an hour before she'll expect a briefing. It's not that I don't want to see you again. It just can't interfere with my work."

He quirked a brow and his mouth twisted as if he were reluctant to admit she'd scored a point.

"Honestly, Axel, I knew she was coming today. I just didn't know she was flying and would be here so soon."

She came to sit beside him. "You must think… Well, I don't know what you think."

He turned toward her and stroked her hair, which was still tangled and as wild as he knew she could be. Then he drew her in and she let him. He dropped a kiss on her forehead before stepping away. He took the opportunity to stroke her cheek with his thumb. His touch sent an electric tingle over her skin.

"Let me know if you need anything from Onutake County."

She held her smile. "I'll be in touch."

Then she headed for the door, one hand shoved in her jeans pocket, clutching the key to her motorcycle. In her back pocket, she'd shoved her nearly dead phone. She needed to get to the motel to recharge its battery and her own.

Something popped into her mind and she paused at the door to his bedroom. He watched her, his dark brows lifted.

"Um, I think I'll be going out to the Eternal Wisdom commune today. Maybe I can find some reason to shut them down."

His expression grew stormy and the blood vessel at his neck pulsed dangerously. "Not alone. We discussed this."

"They might be involved in smuggling."

He snorted. "If they are, you'll never catch them."

"And why is that?"

"Too smart."

She picked up the gauntlet he'd tossed. "We'll see about that, won't we?"

"You aren't going alone."

"I'll have my team with me."

"They don't know these people like I do."

"You can ride along, if you like."

The acid in his empty stomach burned at just the thought of going out there with her because he knew that Father Wayne would instantly pick up the vibe between them. Then he would delight in revealing to Rylee that he was Axel's father.

The only thing worse than having that happen was letting her go out to that place without him. She didn't know or understand how very dangerous Father Wayne could be.

His breathing changed, coming in short angry puffs, and his teeth were locked so tight he'd need the Jaws of Life to get them open.

Axel considered and decided that his shame was small compared to Rylee's safety.

"Axel? You all right?"

He unlocked his jaw. "I'm going with you. End of story."

"Okay, let me clear it with my supervisor. I'll get back to you." She glanced at the screen of her phone. "Jeepers. I have to go."

He walked her out and watched as she drove off, knowing he would have to tell her. Father Wayne was more than a cult leader and con man. Rylee had the right to know. His father was why he stayed and, more specifically, because of what he feared his father might do. Axel was imprisoned here as surely as when he had been trapped behind the congregation's walls. He had to stay, to be here to stop his father from ever carrying out his deadly version of the Rapture, which he called the Rising.

LIEUTENANT CATHERINE OHR waited for Rylee in her rented sedan outside a craftsman-style home painted gray. Rylee checked the address again and pulled behind her boss. The two women exited their vehicles simultaneously.

Lieutenant Ohr swung the leather briefcase over one shoulder as she cleared the distance toward Rylee with her long stride. She extended her hand and the two women shook.

"Right on time," said Ohr. "We are gleaning some interesting data from the drone. Good work on its recovery."

"Thanks," said Rylee. "I had some help with that. Wouldn't have gained access to the survivalist camp without the assistance of the sheriff."

Her supervisor's mouth turned down. Ohr was a tall woman, nearly six feet in height, and she was skeletally thin. Rylee had observed her at lunch; generally, Ohr ate a cup of yogurt at her desk and seemed to leave her computer only to smoke cigarettes. As a result, her complexion was sallow and her brown hair thinning and brittle. The lines around her mouth, always prominent, seemed to harden at the mention of the sheriff.

"Yes. Sheriff Trace. I read that in your report. It's generally a good idea to cooperate with local law enforcement. However, in this case, I think you might have done better to speak to the former sheriff, Kurt Rogers. Better information and less entanglements."

Rylee's brow wrinkled and confusion settled over her, along with a twinge of anxiety. Why would she have spoken to the former sheriff? And what entanglements did she mean? Was she talking about her personal relationship with Axel? But how would she know?

Lieutenant Ohr paused on the sidewalk to face Rylee.

"This is where Kurt Rogers lives," said Ohr. "He has some information on Sheriff Trace that I think you need to hear. Shall we?" Ohr motioned toward the house and did not wait for Rylee before extending her long legs and striding up the walkway to the front door. She ignored the bell and knocked briskly. As they waited, her supervisor tightened the sash on her leather jacket. A deep bark told Rylee a large canine had come to the door. Then there was a voice of someone telling the dog to be quiet and a moment later the door swung open.

The man had a full white mustache, rosy cheeks and hair that made Rylee think for a moment that he perhaps belonged at the North Pole. He was slim, however. But the choice of suspenders to hold up his jeans did reconfirm her initial impression. The man looked from one to the other, swept them each with a glance and said, "I see the dress code hasn't changed. But the last time I spoke to the feds, they were both males, so perhaps we are making some forward progress. Come on in, ladies."

He stooped to grab hold of the collar of his black Lab, whose thick tail thumped against his master's leg. Rogers told his dog to sit and she did, her tail now thumping on the carpet runner as the two women stepped inside. Catherine ignored the canine, but Rylee extended the back of her hand to the dog, allowing the animal to take in her scent.

"This is Ruby," said Rogers. The dog's ears perked up at the mention of her name. Rogers released her and she stayed where she was until he guided them from the entry to the living room, at which time she took the opportunity to sniff the legs of both new arrivals before settling in a dog bed beside the recliner.

After the initial chitchat, they were motioned to a sofa. Rogers chose the well-worn and stained brown leather recliner.

"I understand you want some background information on the current sheriff. That right?"

Her supervisor not so much sat as perched on the edge of the sofa, ankles together and hands clasped on her knees.

"I wondered if you could fill in my subordinate on what you told me on the phone and include any additional details you might have recalled." Catherine tapped her clasped hands together as she spoke.

Rogers drew a long breath and then turned to Rylee. The pit of her stomach dropped, and she felt the tightening of the muscles between her shoulders. Whatever he was about to say, she knew it was not good. What would these two think if they knew she had come directly from Sheriff Axel Trace's king-size bed to this meeting? Rylee repressed a shudder.

"Well," said Rogers. "I told Ms. Ohr here that Axel used to walk to Kinsley whenever he could slip away. He didn't talk much but the librarian sort of took him under her wing." He turned to Catherine at this and continued with, "She's retired now, as well. But I can put you in touch, if you'd like. I'm sure she may have some additional information on Axel."

"Not necessary for now."

Rogers turned his attention back to Rylee. "He didn't really fit in with the people. I could see he was unhappy and it bothered me that no one came looking for him. No matter how long he was gone. That got me to call social services. We all went out and had a look at the compound."

Rylee sat forward as if stabbed in the back. Had he said compound?

"Other than their unconventional living situation, we did not find the children in poor health or malnourished. All of them seemed relatively happy and…" Rogers rubbed his neck. "You know, they just have different ideas. Ideas that I'd call dangerous. And not everyone out there toes the line. One of Reverend Wayne's followers was arrested by Border Patrol for transporting an Eastern European into the US."

"A Croatian," said Ohr.

"Leadership denied knowledge and I found nothing to prove otherwise."

"Do you feel they are engaged in human trafficking?"

"Maybe. Might have been an outlier. I couldn't catch

them, but for that one time. If folks at the compound are smuggling or trafficking, I never found any evidence."

Rylee interjected here. "You say *the compound*. What exactly are you referring to?" But she knew. She was certain that she already knew.

Rogers brows lifted. "Oh, I thought you knew. Axel was born on the lands belonging to the Congregation of Eternal Wisdom. His dad is the leader of that group. Man named Wayne Trace. Goes by Reverend Wayne."

"His name isn't Trace. It's Faith."

"Changed it."

Ohr gave Rylee a long, critical look. "Thorough background check would have revealed the name change."

Rylee dropped back into the thick padding of the seat cushions. Wayne Faith was Wayne Trace. Cult leader and Axel's father. If she was such a crack investigator, how was it possible that she had missed this?

The knot in her stomach turned into a whirling sea, pitching so hard that she needed to grip the armrest to steady herself.

One of the men on her watch list was the father of the sheriff. How much worse could it be? She knew the answer to that. She could have slept with the son of a man who was about to go on her list of suspects. That would make it worse.

Rylee's supervisor lifted a brow, regarding her. "Is something wrong?"

Rylee forced herself to release the armrest and managed to give her head a shake. She turned her gaze to the former sheriff. She put aside her emotions, pressing them down deep where they threatened to explode like compressed gas. "Mr. Rogers, the sheriff gave me some information on this group, but I would appreciate it if you could you tell me exactly what you mean when you say they have dangerous ideas."

Rogers thought for a minute. His index finger setting the whisker straight in his mustache.

"Yes, I could do that."

Chapter Sixteen

Axel waited for Rylee on the shore of St. Regis River in a park that was a popular launch for small crafts. He suspected that she'd set the location because she did not want to be seen with him. He didn't blame her. He should have told her the truth, even knowing that this was exactly what would happen.

Most women did not like being lied to, but this omission interfered with her case. Could she forgive him?

Maybe she doesn't know. Which meant that she would find out eventually or that he had to tell her.

He liked neither option. They'd already gone too far. His night with Rylee had made him wonder about things that he had no right thinking about. Like what it would be like to wake up to see her in his bed every morning.

I'll bet she'd be a great mom.

Axel wiped the sweat from his upper lip. That was the kind of thinking that was going to get his heart broken.

What was he doing? He would be a terrible father. The only examples he had of parenting were twisted. All he really knew was what not to do. Could that be enough?

He was out of his unit now without remembering

leaving his SUV. He paused in his pacing to look back at his vehicle, the door open and the alarm chiming. He strode back to slam the door. Then he faced the water. The fog was thicker there, rolling toward him like some special effect in a stage production.

This park was too close to the compound of the Congregation of Eternal Wisdom for his liking. The compound was situated on the St. Regis River. Mid-river lay an island belonging to the Kowa tribe, and the shore beyond was also Mohawk land. Beyond that, across a narrower stretch of the St. Lawrence, lay Canada.

Axel shifted, rocking from side to side as he stood between his vehicle and the river. If not for the fog, he could have seen the fence just south of this spot. One had to have lived there to know it wasn't to keep intruders out so much as it was to keep insiders in. He hadn't been back to this spot since the day he'd jumped that fence and walked out that last time.

The cold of the air and the warmth of the water had created a real London-style fog, but the chill he felt had nothing to do with the damp or the fact that he could not see more than fifty feet. He didn't need to see, it was all there in his mind—the layout, the women and children in one building, single men in another and the others, the ones they called most blessed, ensconced in their own house. These were the ones who had made, what his father called the greatest sacrifice, and what Axel called self-mutilation.

The engine sound brought him around. Headlights glowed eerily in the mist. Tires crunched on gravel and he recognized her sedan, the red handprints nearly unnoticeable in the mist. She parked her car at an angle, so her departure would not require her to reverse direction. Her cab light flashed on as she exited her car, shutting her door with more force than necessary.

She paused to lock her car, unnecessarily, he knew. Then she cinched the belt to her coat before marching toward him. One of the large boulders, placed to keep folks from accidentally driving into the river, gave him support as he sagged.

Her expression told him all he needed to know. She knew everything. He could see it in the upward tilt of her chin and the downward tug at the corners of her mouth.

She stopped and glared. Her face flushed. He forced himself not to shift as he held her cold stare.

"I don't even know where to begin," she said.

"I'm sorry, Rylee. I should have told you."

"Yeah! My first field assignment and your father is on my watch list."

"He wasn't. You never mentioned him."

"But you knew that he should be. You knew that one of his followers was arrested by Border Patrol for transporting an Eastern European into the US."

"A Croatian. My father denied knowledge."

"Do you believe him?"

"It doesn't matter what I believe. Only what I can prove."

"It matters to me."

"Part of the indoctrination is to believe that he is one of God's chosen. I believe that none of his followers would take such action without his specifically ordering them to do so. I told ICE exactly that when they questioned me."

Immigration and Customs Enforcement had charged one of Reverend Wayne's followers, William Evers, with human trafficking. The illegal immigrant was deported and, as far as Axel knew, Evers was still in federal prison.

"You lied to me," she said.

"I omitted."

"You were born there, in that compound. I'm looking for a foreign agent on US soil and now I learn that one of your father's followers was engaged in human trafficking. That kind of activity points to the possibility of ongoing human trafficking. The sort of trafficking that might bring my suspect to your county."

"Do you have evidence to that effect?"

"We know a foreign agent carried a deadly virus strain onto US soil. We know that person is missing. Additionally, we know that one of Wayne Faith's followers once transported an Eastern European illegally into this county. And we know that you are the son of Wayne Trace, whose surname was changed to Faith. Do you have any idea what my affiliation with you will do to my career?"

"Who you sleep with is your business, Rylee."

"The trouble is I don't really know who I slept with. Do I?"

He glanced away.

"It's not just that you lied, Axel. It's that I can't trust anything you say, or don't say, again."

He looked back at her. "You ever been ashamed, Rylee? During your years traveling with your family or in college or maybe in your stellar career? You have someone in your past that you'd do anything to distance yourself from?"

"If you wanted distance, why did you move back here after your discharge?"

It was a question he didn't think on because the answers hurt too much.

"Maybe I wanted to be near my mother."

"Who is?"

He looked away again. "I don't know. But if she ever wanted to leave, I wanted her to know I was close. That I could help her if she'd let me."

"Is that all?"

He looked up and then to the river and then to the ground. Everywhere and anywhere but at Rylee.

"Why else, Axel?"

"To stop him. I wanted to be here in case he set a date. I have siblings there. I have childhood friends who never left. If Father Wayne decides that the Rising is coming, I wanted to be here to stop him."

"Stop him from what, Axel?"

"They rehearse their departure to Heaven's Door. That's what he calls mass suicide. Not death, just a door. They have costumes and rituals. He holds their lives in his hand. On his word, they'll all kill themselves."

He hazarded a quick glance to see Rylee's mouth had dropped open.

"Can't you close them down?"

"I told you, I've tried. It's not illegal to believe what they believe. I've had Child Protective Services out there dozens of times. The children show no signs of abuse. And their upbringing is no harder than Fundamentalists or any number of religious subgroups."

"His religious beliefs are crazy."

"But not illegal."

She closed her mouth and gave him a troubled stare. She seemed to be deciding something. Axel held his breath. When she didn't speak, he broke the silence.

"If you have something on him, some law that he's broken, I can help you."

Rylee shook her head. "Perhaps you do really want to stop him. I don't know. But you can't be involved in this investigation any longer and I cannot have anything more to do with you."

"Rylee, please."

"Goodbye, Axel." She started to turn away.

He felt the panic squeezing his heart. He couldn't breathe. Axel's hand shot out and he stopped her, drawing her back.

"You can't tell me you don't have feelings. That what we shared meant nothing to you."

"I can't say that. But I can say it is the reason why this hurts so much. You made a mistake. I can forgive you. But it's over between us. I can't take the chance that you are holding back other secrets or that my association with you won't jeopardize this case. It's too important. Far more important than either of us."

"Then let me help you," he begged.

"Too late for that, Axel. You know it. Now let me go."

He didn't want to. But he did, releasing her and with her, the best chance he'd ever had at a normal life with a woman who made his body quake and his heart sing. Now, both seemed to be burning to ash. What right did he have to a woman like her, anyway?

Axel watched her go back to her sedan. The engine purred to life and she rolled away, looking straight ahead, as if he didn't even exist. In a moment, the fog made her, and her vehicle, disappear.

AXEL STOOD AT his office window in the building that held all city offices, including his. Right on time, the charcoal gray sedan arrived driven by an unknown female agent with Lieutenant Catherine Ohr in the passenger seat. Behind them, a second car pulled in, this one announcing Border Patrol. Two officers exited, one male and one female, in uniform. He knew them both. Captain Sarah LeMaitre and Officer Greg Perhay. They'd worked the Ogdensburg Bridge and the forty-eight miles of US coastline along this posting for as long as he'd been sheriff, and today their expressions were all business.

Ohr exited the vehicle and headed across the parking area with the second agent in tow. He lost sight of them as they rounded the building. It gave him time to return to his desk and the computer and the mobile phone that still had no texts or messages from Rylee, despite his making three unanswered calls to her.

The two women appeared in the hallway, visible from his office through the glass panel, and entered, coming to a stop before him in the small seating area beyond his desk. In the hallway, LeMaitre and Perhay flanked the entrance. Axel's unease grew as he turned to his visitors.

Ohr wore a business suit and black leather trench coat with the collar upturned, bright red lipstick and a low-heeled shoe. She was gaunt, even with the coat adding much-needed bulk. Her cheekbones stood out and the makeup she used did not hide the unhealthy color of her complexion.

The second agent, by contrast, was tall and fit with brown skin and dark curling hair clipped close to her head. She wore a thigh-length blue woolen coat with an upturned collar, gloves and a cashmere scarf the color of oatmeal.

Ohr shook his hand. Her long bony fingers clasping his for the briefest time possible. Then she introduced the second agent, Lucille Jackson.

"What can I do for Homeland Security?" he asked, wondering why Rylee was not here with them but unwilling to ask.

"I understand from Kurt Rogers that you were born on the compound of the Congregation of Eternal Wisdom," said Ohr. She might as well have slapped him across the face.

His cordial smile slipped and he straightened, feeling the need to sit down.

"Yes. That's correct." He motioned to the chairs before his desk. "Would you care to sit down?"

Ohr gave a shake of her head but not a hair moved. She stepped in, crowding his personal space.

It was a technique of which he was familiar, and so he forced himself not to step back. She smelled of ash and tobacco. He glanced to Jackson, who had a pad of paper out and was jotting down notes.

"Are you still a member?" asked Ohr.

"No. There are no members outside of the compound. You are either in or out."

"Emancipated at thirteen?" asked Jackson.

"Yes." Axel did not like being on this side of the questioning.

Ohr leveled him with a steady stare. "We have reason to believe that the individual who escaped capture on Monday, September 4, may be here on Congregation's property."

He straightened. "Your source?"

"I'm not able to share that. The message was received by a Border Patrol agent." She lifted a hand and motioned to the agents behind her without turning her head.

Captain LeMaitre stepped forward and handed over the letter, which Ohr passed to Axel. The page was torn from a lined composition book. He recognized the type of paper from his early schooling on a twisted version of the world beyond the compound walls.

He read the note.

The Rising is near. We are prepared and joyful to reach Heaven's Door. Please tell our son, Axel, we will miss him and have missed him greatly. Ask him to come home to us.

"Where did you get this?" he asked.

"One of the brothers from the congregation delivered it to a border agent. Do you want to tell me what this means?" asked Ohr.

"This congregation believes that they are the chosen people and that a great disaster is imminent."

"And they'll be spared?" asked Jackson, her eyes rolling toward the ceiling as if having heard this on too many occasions.

"The opposite. They believe they will be called to

the Lord before the Desolation. They prepare by ready-ing themselves to meet God by living according to their leader's mutation of religious scripture."

"Mutation is an interesting choice of word," said Ohr.

Axel absorbed this gut punch with only a twitch of his brow. She knew about the rituals of castration, then?

Ohr smiled and extended her hand for the note. He returned the page, folded as it had been.

"There's something else," said Axel. "Part of their ceremonies are preparations for the Rising. If Father Wayne tells them the Desolation is near, it is possible they might all take their lives."

"You are talking about mass suicide?"

"I am."

"I'm aware of their beliefs. Unfortunately, shutting down this organization is not our objective. We are not interested in another Waco. My objective is recov-ery of the foreign agent who slipped through Agent Hockings's fingers." She tilted her head in a way that was birdlike. "Are you certain Wayne Trace is your father? I understand that he gives all children born on the compound his name. Isn't that correct?"

"That is because all the children born in the com-pound are his. He is the chosen one. The only man al-lowed to touch the women. That means any and all women of age."

Ohr folded her arms as if finding this unsettling. Her expression showed her disapproval. "Your mother is there?"

"As far as I know."

"What is her name?"

It was such an obvious question. But the answer

made him sick to his stomach. He wrinkled his nose and swallowed. Trying not to look at Ohr, he spoke.

"I don't know her name. The women who elect to join the cult, they are not allowed to claim their children. All those born there are separated from their birth mother and raised communally by women who have not yet born children or are past the age to bear children."

Ohr's brows rose high on her forehead. She and Jackson exchanged a look. He recognized the silent exchange, having witnessed it before—pity mixed with disgust.

"Why is that?" asked Ohr.

"Part of Reverend Wayne's dictates. Children belong to everyone."

"During your time there, did you ever see any illegal activities?"

"No."

"Funding?"

"Donations to his cause and the assumption of all assets from those who decide to throw in with him."

"You know what Agent Hockings recovered here. You know that we are still in pursuit of the person who transported this package. Our investigation leads us to the conclusion that this individual is still in your county. In your opinion, would your father have any reason to shelter such an individual?"

"Don't call him that."

"But Reverend Wayne Trace *is* your father."

Axel lowered his head. The truth was impossible to bury. He knew because he had tried. He took a moment to breathe, the air heavy with the stink of stale cigarette smoke, and then he answered her question.

"He's been preaching the coming apocalypse, the end of the days, for nearly twenty years now. That's a lot of days gone and his followers all willing and wanting to meet their maker. Eager, even. The outbreak of a plague would give his prophecies more credence. Earn points with his followers. Maybe bring in a pile of more followers. So, yes. I believe it is possible that he would assist and shelter such an individual."

"Our findings exactly. We have the layout and all the information on known members within. What I need from you are details on the life inside and the interior layout of buildings to which we might need access. Drone surveillance shows us that one individual never leaves the women's compound. Is that normal?"

"No. Every one of the members have work assignments. The only exception is illness."

"Thank you."

Axel wondered who was ill or injured. Then another thought struck him.

"Do you think this person, in the women's compound, is the one who transported your package?"

"Not at liberty to say," said Ohr. "Now, your congregation hosts retreats for outsiders."

"It is not *my* congregation."

"Yes. In any case, they allow outsiders in for up to three weeks."

"But they are housed in a separate area."

"For the most part. But not during meals."

"If they wish to join the congregation for prayer or meditation or meals, they are welcome," said Axel. "The congregation makes their way of life look ideal. Pastoral, simple. Wayne is a very charismatic guy and he knows how to sell the soap."

"Soap?"

"His lifestyle. The congregation. Most of the converts are unhappy people who have been on more than one retreat. Folks who don't fit in anywhere else, I guess. He makes the unhappiest among them feel a part of things until they just let go of their old life and join him."

The possibility hit him like a fillet knife to his stomach. He braced as he looked from one woman to the other.

"Which brings me to our next concern. We need to identify the residents there. Do you have a list of some sort?"

"I'm sorry, I don't."

"Then we need agents inside. Drones can only do so much. The members never look up, so there is no way to identify any of the residents. Damn bonnets, hats and veils. And if they are hiding someone, our suspect, we need access to find him."

"You think they'll walk your agents to the very spot where they might be hiding someone?"

"That's the mission. We don't require their cooperation."

"I could assist."

"Your connection with this group makes that impossible. But we will inform you when operations are complete." With that announcement, the lieutenant turned and left his office. Jackson fell in beside and slightly behind her.

"How much personnel do you have up here?" he asked the retreating figures.

"I'm not at liberty to say."

"Because he's got fifty or more. And he's got contacts."

"Who do you mean?"

"The North Country Riders. That adds another thirty. You are badly outnumbered. I'd advise against charging into the lion's den."

"You are being dramatic. They're federal officers. They can handle themselves."

Axel knew his sire was fully committed to his little empire. What he didn't know was what he was capable of, when his kingdom was threatened.

Would he follow through and call for the deaths of all his followers? Would they do as he commanded, go to their bunks and take the cocktail of drugs inducing a sleep from which none would ever awaken?

Axel found himself on the move without even recalling leaving his office. He had to speak to Rylee.

Chapter Seventeen

Rylee looked from one woman to the next. Each wore a brown head covering that allowed her to see no part of her hair color. Their complexions ran the gamut from a deep walnut to a freckled pink. But they all shared the same cautious eyes and rigid posture.

The meeting with Reverend Wayne Faith had not gone well. The man talked in circles, repeating himself and the same quotable truisms.

God's hand will bring justice.

We are the chosen.

This life is the true path to Heaven's Door.

We pray for the souls of the lost.

By the lost, he included Rylee and all who lived outside the walls of his compound.

It was just past 5:00 p.m. on Saturday night and she and Agent Lucille Jackson stood before his stylish desk surrounded by murals depicting people dressed in shapeless brown garments being lifted into the sky. The Rising, he had explained in detail. The mechanics of which seemed to involve the trigger of a great human disaster followed by God welcoming home only these few men and women. She'd have laughed if they were not all so serious and deadly sure. What she didn't know was if the good reverend would be willing to give his predicted apocalypse a little shove forward by helping to smuggle into their country a population-decimating virus.

"We will need to see the living quarters," said Agent Jackson, keeping her voice calm while revealing a bit of the southern accent. She had not removed her mirrored glasses and so the stare down was one-sided.

Rylee's fellow agent stood five inches taller and had clear brown skin with russet undertones. She wore her black hair close-cropped and an impenetrable expression.

The standoff stretched, tight as a stretched rope.

Finally, Wayne spoke. "It would be out of the question to allow two women into the men's quarters."

Rylee had elected to wear a DHS ball cap, in deference and as a reminder of who and what she was. No need to announce or explain to his followers. They likely already knew she was a federal agent. Whether that would attract or repel was an open question.

"We will start with the women's quarters, then," Rylee said and turned to go.

Wayne hurried around his desk. The man was thin with a fleshy face and neck that would make a tom turkey proud. His hair was sparse, but he had grown the back out and wore it braided in some aberration of the elves of Middle-earth. Unlike his followers' drab attire, Wayne's robes were white. The rest of his congregation wore the more practical brown, which was perfect for the thaw that turned the icy roads here into a muddy quagmire.

He managed to get ahead of them as they reached the lobby beside his office and before his church of death.

"You can't go alone."

"Federal officers," drawled Agent Jackson. She waited as Wayne scowled and stared at his reflection in her glasses. Now his gray complexion had a healthy flush. The man was not used to being challenged. That much was clear.

"An escort, then."

"If they can keep up," said Jackson and headed outside.

Rylee was glad for the hiking boots that remained on despite the sucking mud.

Jackson swore as she lifted her pant leg to reveal a shoe and sock smeared with what Rylee hoped was only mud. There were farm animals wandering about.

Before they had reached the women's quarters, a young female dashed up before them, arms raised to stop them.

Jackson had her hand on her sidearm. "You do not want to do that," she warned.

"Sister Della is coming. She's right there." The woman's wave had changed to a frantic combination of pointing and motioning.

Jackson kept her attention on the young woman and her hand on her weapon while Rylee glanced back the way they had come.

Striding toward them from the stables was a tiny stick of a woman who held her skirts high to avoid the mud. The result was a troubling view of her striped socks and rubber clogs below cadaverous knees. She moved quickly for one so small. Rylee judged her to be in her fifties from the heavily etched lines around her mouth and the fainter ones around her eyes. Unlike her pale legs, her face was ruddy and tanned as if she spent every minute of the day out of doors.

"That's her. Sister Della is an elder," said their obstructer. "She'll take you in."

The woman lifted a hand. "Sister Nicole, I am here. What is the trouble?"

"These two demand access to the women's quarters," said Sister Nicole.

"Demand? Not a pretty start. Ask, children. Just ask." She reached beneath her robes.

"Stop," said Jackson.

Della did and cast her a curious expression. Rylee cocked her head as she stared at familiar blue eyes and that nose… She recognized this woman but was certain they had never met. Had they?

"What are you doing?"

"Getting my keys, girl."

"But slowly," said Jackson, her weapon now out of the holster.

The woman's face did not register fear so much as fury.

"You bring weapons into this holy sanctuary?" asked Sister Nicole.

"We are federal officers and we carry guns," said Rylee.

Sister Nicole tugged at her brown garments, looking affronted. Sister Della lay a hand on the younger woman's shoulder.

"I'll take them from here," said Sister Della.

Sister Nicole opened her mouth as if to raise an objection and then acquiesced, nodding and lowering her gaze. She lifted that gaze to glare at the intruders before returning the way she had come.

Sister Della watched her, the smile on her face peaceful as a summer sky. Then she slowly withdrew the keys. "I'll take you anywhere you wish."

Jackson pointed at the women's quarters and Sister Della led the way. Over the next hour, they wandered in and out of stables, gardens, residences and any outbuilding large enough to hold a shovel. Sister Della gradually lost the reclusive reserve and asked Rylee a few questions about herself and her beliefs.

"Are you enjoying your time here on the St. Lawrence?"

"Working, mostly."

"Have you met our son, Axel Trace?" asked Sister Della.

"Our?" asked Jackson.

"Children belong to all of us," she explained. "We were grieved when he joined the army and now, a sheriff, still using weapons to solve the world's problems. What he never understood is that there is no saving the world. Only yourself—your soul must be clean, you see."

"I have met him," said Rylee.

"Have you? What does he look like?"

Clearly, Axel did not visit.

"Would you like to see a photo? I have one on my phone."

"On a phone? Really?"

She looked mystified, as if she had never seen a mobile phone.

"How long have you been inside these walls, Sister?" asked Rylee, as she pulled up the photo she had taken of Axel and Morris Coopersmith on the bench outside the ice-cream stand her first night in town. She wasn't sure why she had kept the shot instead of deleting it. Axel looked relaxed and had a gentle, sweet smile on his face as he sat with his head inclined toward Morris. Looking back, she realized that it was the first moment when she began to fall in love with Axel.

Sister Della moved in as Rylee stared at Axel's kind, handsome face.

"Hockings? You all right?" Jackson asked.

Rylee shook her head and turned the phone, so the sister could see. Sister Della opened both hands and placed them on either side of the phone, cradling his image and Rylee's hand.

"Oh, he's so handsome. Looks just like his father," said Sister Della.

Rylee glanced back at the image. She didn't see the resemblance between Axel and Reverend Wayne. And she was certain that Axel would do anything to change his lineage.

Sister Della sighed and released Rylee's phone, pressing both hands over her heart. "He looks well."

"He's a strong, capable man." *Despite your efforts*, she thought.

"We've only had three leave us. All boys and all to the army. Can you comprehend? We are pacifists. Killing is against God's law."

"What about killing yourself?" asked Jackson.

"Do you refer to the Rising? That's not killing, Lamb. That is responding to the call of our Lord."

Della's placid smile was disturbing. Rylee shifted uncomfortably in the austere quarters.

"Has the sheriff been helping you to find what you seek?" asked Della.

Rylee took a chance. "He is. We are looking for a person. Foreign national, likely Chinese."

"Really? Here? I've seen no one like that." Her face was troubled and Rylee sensed she did know something.

"Axel has been searching with us. It's important to him."

"What has he done, this Chinese person?"

"He's a threat to national security," said Jackson.

"National." She laughed. "There are no nations. We are all one." The sister turned to Rylee. "May I see that photo again?"

"I can make a copy for you."

"Really? I'd like that. Though we are not supposed to have photos of—well, yes, but he's not my old family, so perhaps… I'm not certain." After this conversation with herself concluded, she beamed at Rylee. "I'd like that."

Dark clouds continued to build throughout the late afternoon. As the sun dipped, so did the air temperature.

"Are there any other buildings on the compound?" asked Jackson, now shivering from the cold and casting a glance skyward.

"None here." Despite her small stature, Rylee thought she noticed the sister straightening, growing and setting her jaw.

"What is it?" asked Rylee.

"Have you been down to the river?"

"Yes. Do you mean here on your grounds?" Rylee was not looking to the north toward the St. Lawrence but to the west, where the St. Regis River glinted steel gray through the trees.

"That river is a dangerous waterway. We only use our boats in fair weather."

"Boats?" said Jackson. "Here?"

"Yes, they are outside of the compound but belong to Father Wayne. Some of the male members of our congregation are lobstermen who use the boats daily to check their pots. One of the men at the boathouse could show you."

"What do you use the boats for?" asked Rylee.

"I'm sure I don't know. I'm in charge of the animals. And the women are not allowed near the boats."

A few more questions and they discovered where the boats were located. Sister Della walked them back toward the church and sanctuary, where their car was parked.

"Right through there." She pointed toward the open gate. "If you are quick, you might find your...man."

Rylee didn't like her impish smile, as if she were the only party privy to some joke.

"The road to the boathouse is on the north side of the outer wall, judging from the engine noise I hear."

Sister Della offered a wave before she turned and walked toward the barn and the animals in her care.

"Why did she tell us that, about the boathouse?" asked Jackson.

Rylee shook her head, perplexed. She had been wondering exactly the same thing. But Sister Della had told them something else. She had told them to hurry.

"Boathouse?" asked Rylee.

"Oh, yeah," said Jackson. "Calling in our position and destination," she said, and with that done, they headed to their car and left the compound grounds, turning north to the dirt road that paralleled the high concrete block walls. The afternoon bled into evening, with the gray clouds making the twilight come early. The lights of some buildings beyond the wall and below their position came into view.

"That's right on the river. How did we not see it?" asked Jackson.

"We saw it, but there is no affiliation between that business and this church. I've checked all their holdings. A marina is not among them."

Jackson gripped the wheel over some kidney-jarring ruts and steered the sedan to the shoulder. "Wonder what else Reverend Wayne left off the list."

"Lots of vehicles for this late in the season," said Rylee.

She took out her binoculars. Below them lay a small inlet, cut from the river, with steep banks. On the concrete pad were several cars and trucks and beyond was a metal commercial garage or small warehouse that was likely the marina. Stacks of blue-and-green plastic crates, used to ship live shellfish, lined the docks before a crane. Below the jetty, bobbing in the water, three brightly colored lobster boats were tied.

"What do you see?"

"Looks like a quay with commercial fishing vessels,

wharf, lobster traps and crates to ship seafood." She lowered the binoculars. "We need a drone."

"We need a warrant." Jackson put the vehicle in reverse and glanced in the rearview mirror. The curse slipped past her lips. "We've got company."

Chapter Eighteen

"How many?" asked Rylee as she pivoted in her seat. Behind her, she was blinded by the flashing, bouncing headlights.

"Too many!" said Jackson.

"Can't go back."

"What do you think they want?"

The answer came a moment later, when their rear windshield exploded. Rylee screamed as glass fell all about them, pelting the backs of their seats and flying between them, reaching the cup holders and console.

Jackson did not wait, but stepped on the accelerator, sending them jolting forward down the rough unpaved road to the quay. Their pursuers followed. The distinctive sound of bullets pinging off the rear fender sent Rylee ducking behind her headrest.

"Faster," she yelled. Now more in control of herself, she had drawn her service weapon and removed her safety belt. Pivoting until she faced backward and stared out the shattered rear window at the trucks. The flash of headlights was enough for her to identify four pickups, much newer than the old battered models she had seen within the compound.

These might be from the order or someone else altogether.

A flash of gunfire told her which pickup truck was currently shooting at them. She returned fire and was gratified to see the trucks swerve off the twin ruts of a road and bounce into the wooded area to their right. The crash of metal colliding with the trunk of a tree made her flinch.

The rest came on like wolves pursuing the fleeing deer.

"Both dead ends," said Jackson.

Rylee glanced ahead and saw that Jackson had to either veer to the left toward the concrete pad on which sat a commercial metal storage building or to the right and the opposite side of the canal, where the crane, traps and seafood shipping containers sat on a concrete slab above the three fishing boats moored to the jetty. Between the two and beyond both lay the black water of the channel.

"We can't go back," said Rylee. "We're outnumbered and outgunned."

"Right or left?" asked Jackson.

Both bad choices.

"Left," said Rylee, choosing the metal building and the possibility of better cover.

Jackson turned the wheel, committing them to the side that held the commercial garage. As they approached, Rylee saw that the storage facility backed up to the canal on one side and the channel on the other. The building before them was a two-story structure made of sheet metal. On the front sat two bay doors, each large enough to drive a tractor trailer through, but both bay doors were closed. There were no windows that she could see, except in the side door that flanked the structure. Beside the building sat some sort of scaffolding.

"Aim for a garage door?" asked Jackson.

"Likely locked. Left side?"

"It's too close to the river. We might go off into the water."

"We need cover," said Rylee.

"Going through the garage door?"

There was no way to tell if there's a vehicle parked just beyond that door.

"Side door. Right side."

Jackson's elbows extended as she braced. Rylee could not see why but hugged the back of her seat as the car jolted, scraping the undercarriage. Rylee was thrown against her seat and then into the dashboard behind her. When she regained her position, it was to see the pickup trucks fanning out, surrounding them. The smooth ride marked their arrival on a concrete slab that held parking, the metal building and a scaffolding, she now saw, that held six boats at dry dock, parked one above the other and three across.

"Brace yourself," called Jackson. Rylee had time to pivot in her seat as Jackson swerved, sending them careening in a half circle. Rylee lifted her gun arm, still gripping her pistol as she was tossed against her door. The impact jolted her service weapon from her hand.

They now faced their attackers. Jackson's repositioning would allow their car doors to provide them with some cover as they escaped toward the garage's side door.

Where was her gun?

A glance at Jackson showed blood oozed from her nose, running down her chin and disappearing into the navy blue wool of her coat's lapel.

"We have to get inside."

Jackson and Rylee threw open their doors simultaneously. Bullets ricocheted off the grill as Rylee ducked, her hand going to the floor mat. She flinched as her palm landed on something hard. Shifting, she recovered her pistol. Then Rylee exited through the door toward the back of the vehicle.

Jackson was already at the side door and using the butt of her pistol to smash the window glass. Dangerous, Rylee thought until she saw Jackson slip the safety back off.

Rylee reached her as she stretched her arm through the gap and released the door lock from the inside.

The two women slipped inside. Behind them, machine gun fire erupted, closer now, the bullets shrieking through the metal walls all about them.

"I can't see a thing," said Jackson.

Rylee returned her pistol to her hip holster and retrieved her cell phone, gratified to discover that it worked after the jolting exit.

She swiped on the flashlight app and the beam of light swept their surroundings, disappearing into the cavernous space. The shipping containers beside them were neatly stacked and now she realized they were not shipping containers, but the modern version of the clay pots once used to catch lobsters. The more efficient models were each spray-painted with the owner's number. They rose from the floor to the ceiling.

"They're coming!" Jackson pointed toward the bouncing beam of headlights darting through the open side door.

"We need backup."

"Could we take cover under the dock?" asked Jackson as they backed, shoulder to shoulder, farther into the garage.

"There *is* no dock. It's concrete and the seawall. Only way out of here is across the canal or back the way we came."

"Trapped."

That was it. A succinct one-word summary of their situation.

They were pinned and needed to survive long enough for backup to arrive.

Rylee used her phone to send a text with their situation. Then she hit her contacts list, using the mapping app that would send her location with her message. Finally, she added the names to the group text. First, *Catherine Ohr* and *Sarah LeMaitre* from Border Patrol. She swallowed back her doubt before adding the last name, selecting *County Sheriff Axel Trace*. She held her breath and pressed Send.

"This way," said Rylee.

Jackson hesitated. "If they come through the side door, they'll come through one at a time and we'll have a clear shot."

But their pursuers didn't choose the opening through

which they had entered. The sound of their bullet punching through the metal garage door before them and the sound of men shouting confirmed that. Rylee's decision to move became more urgent.

"They're destroying the garage lock," said Jackson.

"That's Wayne Faith," said Rylee. "I'm certain."

Rylee led them with her phone through the cavernous structure, past two boats in dry dock stacked one above the other on metal scaffolding. Beside them sat empty racks and a winch. Construction equipment, including a Bobcat and a backhoe, completed the vehicles. They'd never get out of here in either one, Rylee knew.

At the front corner, beside the door, Rylee noticed a framed office with large glass windows reflecting her light back at them.

"That's just where I'd look for us." Jackson paused, searching their surroundings. "What about those stacked boats?"

"You want to hide in one of those wooden bottomed boats?" asked Rylee. It was the kind of choice that left no option.

"It's cover. Hard to reach. A tower, easier to defend."

"Depends on how much ammo we have. And how much time we have to hold them," said Rylee.

"You walked right by those boats. They might as well. And it would put us behind them. We might be able to slip past them and to their vehicle."

"We can't slip out of those boats," said Rylee. "The bottom one is ten feet off the ground. The scaffold is metal. We won't be quiet on descent and they have semi-automatic weapons."

"Your alternative?" asked Jackson.

She had none, except the mission. "We need to find the suspect. It's the only proof that this congregation is involved."

"Shooting at us should be proof enough," said Jackson.

"Let's go out the back." Before them were two more large garage doors and a small door to the right.

Jackson glanced toward the rear exit. "No cover. Nothing out there but the seawall and water. Plus, any men that may have come around to block that way out."

"It's dark outside. We might get past them or get out before they block us in."

Jackson gave her a dubious look, but nodded.

Behind them, the front garage door inched upward.

At the back door, Rylee flicked her phone to mute as a reply came in from her supervisor. Then she tucked away her mobile. Jackson called to her in a whisper.

"Help coming?" she asked.

Rylee nodded.

"Look." Jackson pointed to the narrow window flanking the back entrance. "At the boats."

Two of the trucks had peeled off and their occupants were now disembarking from their vehicles. They headed under the floodlight and straight for the boat with the red hull.

"They must have seen us come in here," said Jackson.

Rylee nodded. "So what are they after over there?"

She knew the answer before she saw two men haul

the small dark-haired figure from the wheelhouse of the boat.

Their suspect was getting away.

Behind them came the sound of their pursuers, now inside the garage.

FOR THE PAST ninety minutes, Axel had tried and failed to reach Rylee. He had stopped at her motel, called and left messages. With each passing minute, he grew more certain that she was at the compound. He was on his way there when his mobile phone chimed, alerting him to an incoming text message.

He stared at the glowing screen and the message from Rylee. 10-33 Shooting.

He had his SUV turned in the direction of the address listed, an address he did not know. That troubled him. GPS in his sheriff's unit showed a small private quay on the river road near the Congregation of Eternal Wisdom. Axel started to sweat as he depressed the accelerator, exceeding the speed limit on the winding road.

A 10-33 was a call for immediate help.

When he spoke, it was to the empty car's interior. "If anything happens to her, I'll…" *Be lost*, he thought.

Because he loved her.

Why did it take this, gunfire and the possibility of losing her forever, for him to realize that keeping her safe was more important that keeping his secrets?

Axel made one phone call en route. One to his trusted friend Kurt Rogers.

"She called you?" asked Rogers.

"Text. They are pinned down at the wharf."

"What wharf?"

Axel gave him the location.

"Rylee says there are a three lobster boats moored beyond the congregation walls on the river."

"Theirs?"

"She says so."

"What's your plan?"

"I'm going in and getting them out," said Axel.

"Sounds good."

"Call Sorrel Vasta. Ask for boats. I don't want them getting the DHS suspect over to the Canada side of the river."

"I'll ask," said Rogers, his voice relaying his uncertainty.

Axel knew that the cult was unpopular among the Kowa people because of Reverend Wayne's attempts to recruit from among members of their tribe, and the Mohawk people had resources Rogers just did not have. Specifically, they had watercrafts, all sorts, from fishing vessels to tour boats.

"I'm on my way out there now. See you in a few," said Rogers and disconnected.

Axel's car radio crackled to life. Border Patrol was requesting assistance for DHS officer Hockings and Jackson and reporting they were thirty minutes out.

"ETA in five," he replied. He was driving too fast to text Rylee back. He'd just have to tell her when he saw her.

If you see her.

Gunfire. Rylee pinned at a marina he never even knew existed during all that time inside those walls.

Why had no one ever mentioned a wharf and lobstering operation?

The answer seemed obvious. No one wanted them to know. He knew from the meals he'd had as a child that shellfish, usually crab, was often on the menu. What he hadn't known was what else his father had carried across the St. Lawrence in their little private fleet.

He turned off his lights before reaching the compound. There was no road between Rylee's location on the GPS and the road where he sat. He crept along the narrow country road, approaching the north-side wall of the compound, scanning the weeds to his right, and then he saw it: the obvious tracks of many vehicles and the crushed and broken grass on either side of a rutted road.

He lifted his radio and reported the location of the road. Then he released his rear door. He took only the time it required to toss out a traffic cone and light a flare. Then he was back in his SUV and rattling along the frozen ruts of the road. Temperatures were forecast to dip to the twenties tonight, frost warning in effect. It was a bad time to be in or near the water.

The glow from below the hill alerted him that he was nearing his destination. His heartbeat pounded with his racing blood and his jaw ached from clenching his teeth. He flicked off his headlights and crested the hill.

The beams from the halogen lights mounted on the roofs of the pickups below illuminated the area, making the wharf resemble a Friday night football field. He saw men on the wharf and jetty, all armed with rifles.

A second truck barreled over the hill behind him and he turned to see the familiar turquoise truck of Kurt

Rogers. He stood in the headlight's beam and waved. Rogers was beside him in a moment and out of his vehicle, moving well for a man well past sixty.

"Situation?" asked Rogers, settling beside him with his rifle at the ready.

"Unknown," said Axel. He drew out his field glasses and peered at the wharf.

"Who are they?" asked Rogers.

"Don't you recognize that truck?" asked Axel.

Rogers scanned the wharf using the scope on his rifle.

"Looks like Hal Mondello brought his entire crew. Some on the jetty. Some surrounding that building."

The head of the moonshiners was not visible, but Axel knew his truck on sight.

"All this time I thought it was the North Country Riders," said Axel.

"Makes sense. Fishing vessels would make transport of liquor so much easier. Just meet up with another boat out there and load the crates from one to another," said Rogers, as he continued to scan the area using his scope. "Where's your gal?"

He wished she was his. "Likely inside the garage."

"You best get down there, then," said Rogers, still watching the men through his scope. "You got your gun?"

"Of course."

"You aim to use it?" Rogers gave him a hard look.

"If I have to." But he wondered if it were possible. To again use a gun and kill another man. To save Rylee? He hoped he wouldn't.

"Well, now," said Rogers. "Looks like they are transporting more than booze."

Trace followed the direction of Rogers's attention.

"Look on the jetty beside the yellow boat," said his friend.

On the jetty, two men wrestled a small figure from one of the boats.

"That a woman?" asked Rogers.

The figure was diminutive, dressed in black and fighting for all she was worth against the man holding her.

"The one everyone has been looking for."

"I thought the suspect was a Chinese man," said Rogers.

"Can't be a coincidence."

"They have two choices now. Back the way they came or take the boats." Rogers scanned the scene below.

Mondello's men were all scrambling into one boat.

"Looks like they made their choice," said Axel.

"You gonna let them leave?"

"Absolutely. I'm here for Rylee."

"They're taking that gal," said Rogers, indicating the struggling woman. Two men lifted her between them so that her feet never touched the ground as they hustled her along.

"I'm going down there and finding Rylee."

Axel left the trucks and his old friend, using the darkness to move closer through the underbrush that flanked the road.

Below, the men's captive broke free and ran up the jetty. One man lifted his pistol and shot her in the back. The woman's arms flew up. She staggered, her center of gravity now rolling forward, too far before her legs.

Axel ran through the brush as Rogers swore and

started shooting. His friend's aim was good, taking down the man who had shot the woman in the back.

The second man now swept his rifle wildly, moving to find the position of the unknown shooter. He ignored the woman crawling on the jetty, running for cover as Rogers's second shot missed the man who leaped from the quay to the yellow-bottomed boat.

The men on the quay now had Rogers's position and returned fire as Axel moved quickly down the hill. Rylee's text had come from inside the garage, so that was his destination.

Behind him came the wail of sirens. Their approaching cacophony drowned out the shouts of the men below. Border Patrol had made good time.

The men below fired on Rogers, who had moved behind his truck. Their bullets punctured the front grate.

The men by the trucks now moved en masse toward the boats on the opposite side of the canal from the marina. Hal Mondello, past the age of running, paused by the woman, who had made it to her hands and knees. With a mighty shove from his boot, Mondello kicked the woman from the lip of the jetty and into the icy water of the canal.

A door banged open and he saw a familiar flash of blond hair as Rylee ran from the cover of the garage and across the open ground on the opposite side of the jetty. The men, now on the boats, lifted their rifles.

"No, no, no," he chanted as he raced toward the canal. Above, Rogers's shots sent the men ducking for cover.

"What's she doing?" he muttered.

But he knew. Even before she jumped from the jetty, he knew.

Chapter Nineteen

Rylee had left Jackson behind her as she'd dashed out into the cold autumn wind. Jackson could not swim and their suspect, the key to the entire case, had been kicked into the water.

How deep was the water? How cold?

Feet first entry, she'd decided. To be on the safe side. Nothing worse than breaking your neck on a shallow bottom or a piling hidden beneath the inky surface. She saw them, the men scrambling into the boats, as she'd leaped out in one giant stride to nowhere. She'd recognized one of them.

Hal Mondello had stared back at her with a surprised expression as she'd sailed out over the canal. She'd looked from him to the black water before it swallowed her up.

A thousand needles of ice pierced her skin as she struggled with her sodden clothing and waterlogged boots to reach the surface. River water burned her eyes as she realized that this was not like swimming in a lake in July. This water was deadly.

The steel-toed boots and sodden clothing dragged her straight to the bottom. Panic shuddered over her as she fought the urge to gasp against the cold, knowing that one breath of water would be her last. She tipped her head to look back at the surface and saw only deep threatening darkness. The black of a watery tomb. The razor-sharp terror clawed at her, but she forced herself to crouch on the spongy bottom and release her boots. She could not quite feel the laces, double knotted, because of the numbness of her fingers. But one boot came loose and then the next. But now her lungs burned with the need for air.

Rylee tried to release the zipper of her coat, but failing that, she dragged the entire thing over her head and away. The efforts took her sweater with it. Planting her feet, she prepared to push off the bottom when something brushed her cheek.

The blurry image of a woman's face sank before her, the outstretched, lifeless hand gliding over Rylee's chest. Rylee caught the scream of horror in her throat, keeping the precious, nearly exhausted oxygen in her aching lungs. It was her target, the person of interest. Was she dead?

And would Rylee follow her?

She grasped the woman's collar in one fist, locking her fingers around the fabric like the talons of an eagle. She exploded off the bottom with everything she had, kicking toward the surface she could not see. Now she felt the current, dragging her along and out, she realized, to the river.

Sound returned before the light. Gunfire and shouting. The knocking of the vessels against the floats beside the seawall. She couldn't feel her feet or the woman she thought she held. Had she let go?

No time now. Just air, everything centered around that next breath. Now the blackness was punctuated with sparks of light. The surface approaching or her brain preparing to shut down?

She squeezed her eyes shut and kept kicking, willing herself to break the surface, to live, to see Axel Trace again so she could tell him what she should have said the morning he told her about Reverend Wayne. That Wayne wasn't his father and that she was sorry his childhood was so terrible that he felt he needed to hide where he came from. She should have let him know that she didn't care and that she forgave him for the lie because she loved him.

The water gave way to the night and Rylee gasped, inhaling a full breath of sweet cold air. She forgot to kick and just as quickly sank once more. This time she kept kicking, getting her face above and dragging the body of her target with her, struggling until the woman's face broke the surface. Water streamed from the woman's mouth, and she jerked and spasmed as Rylee continued to kick, just managing to keep them both above the surface in the current's pull.

Greedy. That's what the river was. The water making her choose. Take them both to the bottom or just Rylee's prize. A glance to the quay showed they were sweeping out from the mouth of the canal and into the river.

One of the boats left the channel with her, powered by diesel and heading right for them. Rylee realized they meant to run her down. She imagined the propellers cutting into her flesh, shredding her muscle to hamburger.

Rylee stopped kicking and let the river take her again.

AXEL REACHED THE SEAWALL. The gunfire exchange now slowing as those on the vessel redirected their weapons to the river, searching for the woman who had been kicked into it and the one who had jumped in after her.

How cold was that water?

Deadly cold, he knew.

He could not see Rylee, but it was obvious that they could from the shots they unloaded into the river. Each discharge seemed to tear into him.

Mondello's men were aboard the first vessel, now leaving its moorings, and the men from the congregation now drove back the way they had come, back to the compound, where there would be no escape from federal authorities.

A terrible thought struck him. They had an escape. The Rising. If Father Wayne told his followers that this was the night, how many would end their lives in the way they had so long rehearsed? Go to their bed, take the pills, wait for God to bring them to Heaven.

And remove any and all witnesses.

Terror lifted every hair on his body as he pictured them, and him in the years gone-by, dressing in their white robes, swallowing the placebo and lying on the cots in neat rows, like so much cordwood. The tranquilizers taking them quickly to unconsciousness but this time there would be no waking unless they really did wake at Heaven's Door.

Suicide was against God's will. He had learned this only after leaving—the murdering of one's self was prohibited in the Bible.

Where was Rylee? The lobster boat moved out to

deeper water, the men aboard staring back at him and the vehicles from Border Patrol, no longer seeing any of them as a threat. The distraction was why Axel did not see the fast-moving speedboats approaching behind them.

Axel recognized them instantly. The Kowa tribe used these vessels to give tourists exhilarating high-speed rides on the river and perhaps for the occasional tobacco run to Canada. Before the fishing boat was fully underway, it was surrounded by the Mohawk Nation. Gunfire exploded again, and grappling hooks glinted in the air. Axel turned his attention to the water.

A face broke the surface. Rylee, he realized, holding the other woman by the collar of her shirt. Rylee sputtered and struggled to keep her mouth and nose above the surface as she was swept from the boats and downriver. He ran along the seawall, following her course. In a moment, she'd be right in front of him and then, he feared, gone forever.

Chapter Twenty

Rylee saw the orange ring buoy sailing through the air, over her head and past her. But the rope fell across her shoulder. She tried to grab at it, but her arms were so heavy with her sodden shirt and the cold. Her fingers would not respond to her command to clasp. So she hooked her elbow over the rope and held on. She felt the friction as the rope pulled through her jointed elbow, the pain a relief from the numbing death that stalked her. Someone was trying to save her.

After what seemed hours, the ring struck her. She fumbled to get her arm around the ring but it only dunked and bobbed away. She tried again and the ring upended and then shot farther away. Fear enlivened her efforts. If she didn't get ahold of the ring, she'd die. But to grasp the ring, she needed to release her captive.

Was the woman already dead? The hungry, desperate voice in her head told her to let go and that only made her grip the more determinedly against the impulse. She would not let go. Like one of those snakes she had heard of that locked their fangs and would not release even if their head were severed from their body. Rylee held on and watched the ring being tugged away.

She pivoted back toward the receding seawall. Someone was there, gathering the rope, preparing for another throw. But this time, the ring buoy fell short.

On shore, the man tied the rope around his waist. A spotlight illuminated him. It was Axel, stripping out of his jacket and holster. Tearing off his boots and flinging aside his hat. What was he doing?

The answer came a moment later when she saw him back up and then run on bare feet down the concrete pad and dive far out over the water.

Shouting reached her, cutting in and out as she bobbed beneath the surface and then kicked on weary legs back to snatch a shallow breath. The shivering had stopped. Was that good or bad?

A bright light blinded her. A spotlight. If it was the lobster boat, she was dead. Should she let them shoot her or sink once more?

Rylee's kicks grew weaker and she feared that if she sank this time, it would be her last.

AXEL SWAM OUT to Rylee through the freezing water. He could not see her, but he could see the spotlight from one of the boats from the Kowa Nation. He used it like a homing beam, swimming hard and lifting his head only to mark his progress. Behind him, the ring buoy dragged, made noticeable by the slight tug at his waist as he pulled himself along.

He'd learned to swim in the army. A sinker, his drill sergeant had said—too much muscle and little fat. If he stopped kicking, he sank like a stone. But the only way he'd stop was when he and Rylee were safely back on shore. The light danced just before him, so close he could see the entire circle, but he did not see Rylee.

He grabbed a breath of air and dove. Beneath the surface, the light caught the pale glow of her blond hair and skin, now blue in the artificial light.

Rylee reached out her free hand to him as she sank and he grasped her wrist. Reversing course now, he kicked to the surface, breaking first and gasping in the dazzling white light. He dragged her against him with one hand, pressing his chest to hers, keeping her and the second woman before him as he dragged the rope, hand over hand, behind them. The ring buoy hauled closer and closer until he had it behind Rylee. Beside her, the other woman choked on river water and sputtered. Both women had lips the color of raw liver and the shock of that sight was enough to get him swimming.

Shouts reached him. He turned to see Sorrel Vasta waving and motioning him toward the boat. Axel could not even see the shore past the bright light, but he trusted Sorrel and changed course again.

The motor of the boat engine hummed in his ears and then cut abruptly. A second buoy slapped the water beside him and he looped one elbow through the ring. An instant later, he and his charges were gliding along the choppy water toward the stern.

They reached the ladder. Both women were tugged from his arms by many hands. The light flicked off as Axel tried to climb aboard. His hands were stiff with the cold and gripping was difficult. He crooked his wrists and used them, as he might if wearing mittens, to scale the ladder and reach the stern platform. There he sprawled. Heaving and spent.

Vasta kneeled over him, throwing a blanket across his shivering body.

"Axel? We're heading to Kinsley Marina. Ambulance is waiting to take you all to the ER," said Vasta.

Axel nodded. "R-Rylee?"

"She's breathing. The other stopped. We're working on her. Resuscitation. You sit tight."

The engine roared and the boat tipped, cutting through the water like a blade.

"The other b-bo…" His tongue wasn't working, and the shivering was getting worse. That made no sense. He was out of the water and wrapped up tight.

"We stopped Wayne's men before they got inside the walls of their compound. Father Wayne and eight of his men. Trussed up like grouse. My other boat is taking them in to the Border Patrol guys. Ha! Wait until they see what we brought them. They gonna have to cut us some slack. Maybe have to say thank-you. That might about kill them."

"Rye-lee," he whispered.

"We're taking care of your woman, brother. You just sit tight."

A shout and cheer came from behind him.

Vasta grinned. "We got the other lady breathing again."

RYLEE WOKE UP to the sound of a vacuum cleaner and found that she lay between two air mattresses. Beside her, a freckle-faced red-headed woman, dressed in violet scrubs, checked a machine that blipped and pinged beside the hospital bed.

She noticed her patient was conscious and smiled at

Rylee. "You waking up? Good deal. I'll tell your people. They've been in and out of here, checking on you."

"Where am I?"

"Kinsley General Hospital. I'm Tami, your nurse. You're in our ICU. You came in here about the temperature of an ice pop, but we warmed you right up."

"The woman..."

"The one who came in with you?" Tami grimaced. "She's here, too. Bullet wound and the cold. She has frostbite on both feet. Friend of yours?"

"Not really."

"Good, because they have state police standing right at her cubicle. Whatever she did must be bad. We only get that handling when we treat prisoners from Franklin or Upstate Correctional. What'd she do?"

"Not at liberty—"

"To say." Tami rolled her eyes. "Already heard that one. You with Border Patrol?" she asked.

Rylee shook her head. "Department of Homeland Security."

"Well, I'm eaten up with curiosity. You had a near miss."

Rylee lifted the clear covering on top of her that was swollen with air.

"That's a warming blanket. Got one below you, too. Still trying to bring your core temperature up to normal." She tapped away at her tablet and then smiled at Rylee. "Nothing to eat or drink for you just yet. But soon. Your family has been notified."

"My family?"

She tapped on her tablet. "Father, Colonel Hockings."

She paused there to make a face that showed the title impressed. "In...Guam. Army?" she asked.

Rylee flinched. "Marines."

Tami smiled as if it were all the same to her.

"Where is Axel?"

"The sheriff? Next door." Rylee didn't like the smile on Tami's face as Tami glanced in the direction of the hall. "On my way to check his vitals next, which I would do for free. But when I'm done, who will check mine?" She laughed. Then she pointed at the button clipped to Rylee's bed rails. "Press the button if you need anything."

Rylee waited until the nurse left to pull down the air blanket. Immediately, she began to shake and shiver again. She had so many questions to ask and patience was not her strong suit. But she adjusted the blankets and closed her eyes, hoping the blanket did its work quickly. She had not meant to sleep, but when she next opened her eyes, only the light above her bed was on and the blankets both top and bottom continued to reverberate like a vacuum cleaner.

AT SIX O'CLOCK on Sunday morning, Axel checked on Rylee and then checked himself out of the hospital against the doctor's orders. Damned if he'd miss the biggest case this county had ever seen, lying in a hospital bed under an electric blanket. He wasn't leaving without seeing Rylee, though. He discovered from a familiar nurse in purple scrubs that Rylee had been moved to a private room for security. From Tami, he learned that Rylee had been awake part of last night. All her vitals were good, and she would suffer no ill effects from her dive into the St. Regis. The woman she rescued had not fared so well. He was informed that she would likely loose several fingers and both feet to frostbite. One lung had collapsed from the bullet wound and she had suffered dangerous blood loss. Whether that had caused brain damage was still unknown. She was currently in a medically induced coma to protect her brain as she healed.

The trooper stationed at Rylee's door checked him in. They'd been on many traffic fatalities together, so the ID was unnecessary.

"Do you have any word on what happened at the compound last night?" he asked.

"None. Been here most of the night," said the trooper.

Axel nodded and left him, pausing when he reached Rylee's bed, wondering if he could touch her. All the wires and tubes made him nervous. Even her finger had a pulse monitor clipped on. He leaned down and pressed a kiss to her forehead.

"I'm here, Rylee. I'm going to finish this for you."

Her heart rate accelerated and her eyelids fluttered. He waited, hoping she would open her eyes. But she did not, and he let himself out.

He was just passing registration when the circus came to him. The flashing blue-and-red lights of law enforcement vehicles bounced off the waiting room walls from the windows overlooking the parking lot. He reached the main waiting area when the double doors whooshed open and in marched the federal and state authorities, moving in formation.

Catherine Ohr led the pack. She was flanked by two men in dark suits and black woolen overcoats. All that

was missing were fedoras and they could have been ex-
tras in a Bogart and Cagney movie. Behind them, five
state police officers stood with sullen expressions and
bristly short haircuts, the purple band around their Stet-
sons matching the purple leg-stripe on their trousers.

"That was a speedy recovery," said Ohr. "They told
me you were spending the day." The woman smelled
of cigarette smoke.

"Unfortunately, they didn't clear that with me."

"Just coming to see you," said Ohr, pinning him with
watery blue bloodshot eyes. Rylee's supervisor had had
a long night.

"What a coincidence," said Axel.

"Where's Agent Hockings?" asked Ohr.

"Still in her room, sleeping."

Rylee's boss lifted her thin eyebrows at him, then
flashed her shield and ID at the receptionist.

"You have an empty room?"

They were led to a small exam room. Ohr left the
troopers milling in the hall. She and her two agents now
stood between him and the exit, and for a moment, he
thought they were here to arrest him.

"What happened after I went in the river?"

"Quite a lot. The Kowa Nation captured the Mondellos, who were attempting to flee custody in a lobster
boat. The Kowa had several boats. The fastest brought
you, Hockings and the suspect to Kinsley for treat-
ment."

He remembered that. Speaking to Vasta and wondering if the suspect had died.

Ohr continued her summary. "Border Patrol got the
men fleeing the wharf before they reached their com-

pound. My people raided the compound, but Wayne and his council were not among them."

"They got away?"

"He did not. But he tried. Wayne and his people were in a small motorboat on the river trying to flee the country."

"You caught them."

"The Kowa caught them. Initially with Border Patrol." Her smile was broad. "Wayne is in federal custody along with his council, five men who were with him. Two others suffered gunshot wounds and are here in the hospital. My people are interviewing the men and women from the Kowa tribe. Your retired sheriff is helping with a team at the Mondello property. We have all the Mondellos in custody except the eldest of his sons, Quinton. Still searching for that one. Just about finished up there. We still need a formal interview from Rogers. He seems to know everyone in the county."

"Did you get to the compound? Did you stop them from taking the suicide pills?"

"We did. Thanks to you. You told Acting Chief Vasta before they took you to the hospital. They got the word to us."

He vaguely remembered that.

"Seems your father was going to clean house by ridding himself of anyone in the congregation who might have known what he had been up to."

Axel felt sick to his stomach to be associated in any way with that man. To have him as his father was crushing.

"You saved a lot of lives, Sheriff."

Most important of which was Rylee's. Had he saved

his mother? The empty place in his insides ached. Maybe now he'd learn who she was.

"Is there anything else, Sheriff? I need to check on the condition of the woman Rylee dove in to save from the river," Ohr said.

"I've had an update." Axel relayed what he knew about her condition. "I do have one more question. How did Rylee know about the wharf?"

He'd lived inside that compound and didn't know about it.

"According to Agent Jackson, one of the women in the compound suggested they check there for the suspect."

He frowned. It was unlike any of the members to act in a way that would threaten the group.

"Who?"

Ohr referred to her notes again and read. "Sister Della Hartfield."

Della was an elder. Why would she help DHS agents?

"We'll be taking the suspect into federal custody as soon as the paperwork is signed." She motioned to the two agents beside her, who then swept from the room and vanished from his line of sight.

The troopers trailed after them, presumably toward the ICU and their suspect. Axel suspected the doctors and nurses of Kinsley General would put up a fight, but they'd lose.

"Is she the person who carried the duffel?" he asked.

"Yes. Father Wayne confirmed it. He was hiding her at his compound. Waiting, I assume, for the right time to move her. She's the one we wanted. Good work apprehending her."

"I didn't apprehend her. Rylee did that."

Ohr smiled and inclined her chin. "Group effort, then. Retired Sheriff Rogers says that you called him and he called the leaders of the Kowa people."

"That's correct."

"But not Border Patrol. Why is that?"

Axel thought of Rylee's text and his panic at knowing she was in trouble.

"Rylee's text alerted them and you. I called the men and women who I could trust."

"Which included a tribe of Kowa Mohawk and your retired mentor. Not the state police or federal authorities."

"Both too far away to help."

"I should have you fired."

"I'm an elected official."

"Yes. Inconvenient. Likely your county will throw you a parade."

"Probably a pancake breakfast, but I can hope for a spaghetti dinner."

Ohr made a sound in her throat. Then she cleared it and gave him a hard look. "Wayne Faith is your father?"

"So he tells me."

"He's going to prison. Initial overview shows he has offshore holdings and has been playing fast and loose with the congregation's funds for years. In addition to that, as you feared, he called for the followers who remained behind to take some sort of suicide pill."

"But you saved them?"

"Most."

"How many dead?"

"Four. All children. Given the pills before we could reach them."

Axel felt sick.

He turned his back on her and used a paper cup from the dispenser to get some water. The tap water was warm, but it pushed down the bile.

"Additionally, two of Mondello's men were wounded by Rogers. Two Kowas were shot by Mondello's men. No fatalities from the gun battle."

"Who were the wounded?" he asked.

She read the names from a small notebook. He knew each man.

All this, to protect one woman, keep her hidden with his secrets. His father had gone from being a zealot and flimflam man to a federal criminal.

"What will happen to Father Wayne?"

"Espionage charge. It's a capital crime."

Why did he care what they did to him? Was it because he was blood? Blood that had shamed him all his adult life.

"That's why I'm here. Since your father isn't talking."

"Don't call him that."

"Fine. Since Wayne Trace, AKA Father Wayne Faith, isn't cooperating, I need some insight on the congregation. Help sorting and getting those we detained to speak to us."

"He's not even there and he's still controlling them."

"Yes. It's disturbing. He's waiting for an attorney and hoping for some sort of deal."

"Will he get one?" asked Axel, the sour taste in his mouth and pitching stomach now taking much of his attention. Four dead children. He shook his head.

"Not if I have anything to do with it. You all right? You look pale."

He took a few deep breaths, unsure if his condition was physical or a result of being heartsick.

"I'm not all right, but I am willing to help in any way."

She nodded her approval of this.

"We have several members of Hal Mondello's family in custody and are rounding up more of his people. Seems they had some sort of alliance with Wayne Trace. Mondello distributed what Trace smuggled in from Canada, which we, unfortunately, were unable to recover. It's unclear if they knew what they were transporting."

"The duffel Rylee recovered from the Kowa people?"

"That was the second shipment. The first got through. We thought this was the work of Chinese nationals. But that woman you dragged from the river is North Korean. A chemist. We believe Siming's Army was trying to point blame at China, in hopes of increasing tension between nations. That would serve the North Koreans. North Korea would benefit greatly if we lifted sanctions on them while continuing them on China, and even more so if we challenged Chinese control of that region."

"Did you say a chemist?"

"Yes. Possibly here to culture the virus within our borders."

"Culture it where?"

"That's the top question on our list. Most especially if there is a plant currently in operation of this deadly strain of flu as we speak."

That thought chilled.

"But you've stopped them?"

"I'm afraid they don't need the chemist to reproduce what she carried."

"Biohazard?"

"It's a pathogen, Axel. Called a virus seed stock because they use it to propagate more of the virus. Some of it is here. This disease is a powerful killer, the likes of which we haven't seen since the Middle Ages. If it gets loose, we will suffer the worst pandemic ever faced in America."

"A plague?"

"Of sorts. But much, much faster. My experts liken it to the influenza epidemic of 1918."

"But we have the vaccine?"

"Which takes time to produce. In the meantime, we need to find virus seed stock and kill it before Siming's Army can turn that seed sample into an epidemic."

She reached in her pocket, removed a pack of cigarettes and then dropped it back in place. Axel was certain she longed for a smoke. Who could blame her?

"Now, if you would come with me, you can get me up to speed on this cult on the way."

Chapter Twenty-One

Axel had been back within the compound all day speaking to members of the cult individually, with Catherine Ohr there for each interview. The ashtray before her smoldered with the last stubbed-out cigarette.

"Only a few more," she said. "Let's take a break."

They walked out together into the grassy quad. DHS had set up a mobile operations station complete with multiple trailers within the compound's central courtyard. They had even erected a mess hall between the church and living quarters. Generators hummed, powering the mobile light towers that illuminated their way. The entire area now had a distinctly military feel.

Male members of the congregation were being held in the worship hall and the female members were detained in the congregation's dining hall.

As they continued past yet another trailer, Ohr reached for another cigarette and glanced at her phone. "Seven p.m.," she muttered. "I need coffee." She pointed at him. "Want one?"

"Sure."

"They have pastries and coffee in the mess tent. I'll bring you something."

She strode off toward her people, who moved in and out of the buildings, carrying off computers and other bagged evidence.

Agent Rylee Hockings stepped from the sanctuary beside the main worship hall, where he had just been.

"You're here!" he said, sweeping over her and finding her pale and circles under her eyes.

"For several hours now. I've been interviewing the female members of the cult."

They clasped hands and he smiled at her, his heart dancing a percussive rhythm of joy at the sight of her.

"Rylee, you gave me such a scare." He had so much to tell her, to say. He wanted to rush forward and tell her that he loved her and that he wanted her in his life. Then he saw two of his father's men marched past them in handcuffs. The shame of his association with this congregation broke inside him like a drinking glass dropped on ceramic tile. Millions of shards of doubt splintered out in all directions.

"I need to thank you for coming after me. I was losing to the river," she said and gave his hands a squeeze before letting go. Her smile held. "But we got her. Thanks to you. Who knows what we'll learn."

"Ohr told me she's a North Korean national."

"What? Really?"

"She also told me that Sister Della was the one who directed you to the wharf."

"That's true." Rylee was glancing about as if searching for someone. Her supervisor?

"That surprises me," he said. "It seems hard to believe that a congregation elder would do something that jeopardized the group. Any idea why she would do that?"

"Just a theory. I haven't spoken to her yet."

"What's your theory?" he asked.

"I think she did it to help you."

"Me? Why would she want to help me?"

"Ah… I need to find my supervisor."

And just like that, his opportunity fled. Rylee was back on her mission. It would be easier to stop a runaway toboggan than to prevent her from moving forward with her investigation.

There will be other opportunities, he told himself. Better ones, ones when he rehearsed what to say. No woman wanted to be proposed to in a time and place like this.

He could imagine her telling their kids. *Yes, your mother was just out of the hospital after nearly drowning and on her way to interview human trafficking suspects when I proposed.*

He shook his head, dismayed at the ease with which he produced a mental picture of them together with children. What if he waited and there was no other chance?

"Rylee, I need to tell you something."

She was glancing about them now. No longer looking at him, searching, he thought, for her supervisor among the men and women moving across the yard.

"Take a walk with me?" he asked.

"All right. But I have to get back."

"Just a few minutes."

She fell into step beside him away from the aroma of roasting coffee issued from the mess tent. They walked along the worship hall and sat together on a bench that now faced the back of one of the newly placed mobile operation trailers. At least this spot was not directly under one of the many mobile light towers.

He looked toward the empty women's quarters. Already the conversation had veered off track. Rylee was asking about the living situations for the females in the congregation.

"Yes," he said, in response to her question. "The men lived in one building and the women and young children in another."

"But Wayne kept some women in a private enclosure for himself," she added.

"He insisted on celibacy among the males. As for the females, they were celibate, too, for the most part."

"Unless he deemed otherwise," she said and scowled. "They said it was only so they could bring him children. As if that were some high honor." She shook her head, her expression angry. "A blessing, they called it. For the men, castration was the highest show of devotion. For women to be *most blessed*, they needed to give birth."

"Yes," said Axel. Could he have been thinking of proposing to her during this? He must have lost his mind.

"And the males went along with this," she said.

"*If* they wanted to stay. Father Wayne can be very convincing. Made sure it was a status symbol for the males to lop off their junk and the women to sleep with him. Told his followers that it made them closer to God. Prepared to meet the Lord without lustful, earthly thoughts. But I…"

"Did he tell you that?" she asked.

Axel nodded, head bowed and the palm of his hand pressed to the back of his own neck.

"When I turned thirteen, my own father told me that he wanted me to mutilate myself on my eighteenth birthday. It's why I ran."

"What happened?"

"Sheriff Rogers picked me up. He went out there and my father denied the entire thing. He claimed I made the whole thing up, but I know whom the sheriff believed. He told my dad that Child Protective Services would be out there to check every child and regularly. But despite all that, we haven't gotten more than a few children out of their hands."

"They got you out."

He dropped his hand. "It's why I stay. To watch over the children, help the ones who run and make certain he never called for them to enter Heaven's Door. I come out here and I never say when. They let me in because I was a member, hoping, I think, that I would change my mind and come back. As if…" He blew away a breath and then continued. "I'd file a notice of indication with Child Protective Services at any sign the caregivers weren't meeting basic needs. Then I got out with CPS to check the kids with them, make sure they were safe."

"He knew you were watching him."

"Yes."

"It's why they were never harmed."

"Maybe," said Axel. "But he liked having me come back here. I think he knew how hard it was for me. How much I hated it here. And he enjoyed that my leaving caused me suffering and that he'd managed to trap me in this place despite my desertion. He used me as an example of how you can walk away but you can never leave. He says I'm tied to them despite what I might say or do."

"You know, I always thought I had it hard, trying to earn my father's approval. And he could be exacting, difficult, but nothing like yours."

"A fanatic. A con man and now a terrorist. I came from him. What does that make me?" It made him unable to propose to her. That much was certain.

"I can answer that. It makes you the complete opposite. He takes advantage and you protect. He exploits and you defend."

"With him gone, I won't be tied here any longer, Rylee. I can go."

She blinked at him and for a heart-stopping moment, he thought he'd misread her. That what he'd seen as love was just sympathy.

"What about your mother?"

He couldn't even lift his head. "I don't know which one of the women is my mother."

"What do you mean?"

"We were separated at birth. She could not claim me and stay with them."

"There is no *them* anymore. We've been explaining that to the members. They're starting to come to grips with what's happening. Most of them, thankfully, are innocent in all of this. Just misguided."

"What will happen to them?"

"Reconnect with families when possible. We'll process them and release them. Where they go will be up to them."

"Will you help them?"

"If we can." She laid a small hand on his shoulder and he lifted his chin until he met her sympathetic gaze. "Axel? I know who she is."

His heart beat so loud that he thought it might bruise his ribs. "How?"

"She looks just like you. I met her on Saturday, here at the compound. I thought at first that I knew her. It didn't take long to recognize why she looked so familiar. I asked her and she confirmed that she gave birth to you. Would you like to speak to her?"

"Yes!" Axel was on his feet. He leaped at the chance and then thought about confronting a woman who had had many opportunities to reveal who she was—and hadn't. "Maybe you should speak to her first and see if she wants to speak to me."

"All right." She stood and faced him, offering her hand.

"Now?"

Her smile was sympathetic. "Yes, now. They won't be here much longer." She was nearly to the sanctuary's dining hall door when he called her back.

"Rylee? Which one?"

"Della Hartfield."

He blinked and nodded. "Della." It seemed right, somehow. "Do I just wait here?"

"Yes. If she's willing, I'll bring her to you."

Axel raked a hand through his hair and tugged at his shirt, momentarily dragging out the wrinkles.

"You look fine, Axel. Just wait. I'll be right back."

He sat on the bench facing the compound's dining hall as his legs bounced up and down with nervous energy. The next eighteen minutes were the longest of his life. Finally, the door opened and out stepped Della, small and pale, her head still draped in the brown covering she had worn for more than thirty years.

Axel stood. The word tore from him like a cry. "Mom?"

She nodded and swept forward, holding out both hands to him. He took them in something that was not the embrace he had imagined.

He had pictured this meeting so many times, but he was always a boy and she always held him. Instead, this tiny birdlike woman beamed up at him with a smile that seemed to blend contentment with something like madness.

Della had always appeared to have only one foot on the earth and the other somewhere else entirely, as if her spirit was too light to allow her to ever be completely grounded.

She kept him at arm's length as she stared at him. Why had he never seen the similarities until now? Her color matched his, as did her long nose and blue eyes. He pushed back her head covering, expecting to see his blond hair, but her hair was entirely white.

"I'm so sorry that I never defied him. He told me that God would strike you down if I broke my oath and, God forgive me, I believed him." Fat tears coursed down her wind-burned cheeks. Her hands were raw from working outdoors and her spine bent slightly.

"I'm glad my father is under arrest."

Her eyes went wide with shock. "Father Wayne?"

"Yes. I hate him." Hated that he shared the same blood and that his father's deadly legacy would cast a shadow across his heart forever.

Della clasped one of his hands in both of hers and gave a little shake to draw his attention. Then she looked behind her and, seeing only Rylee, she turned back to him. When she spoke, her voice was hushed as if she still feared the retribution of the man who was gone.

"Father Wayne is not your father," she said.

Every nerve in his body fired. Blood surged past his ears and he blinked in stupefaction at her.

"What?" he whispered.

"He's not your father, not really. He claims all the children, but there were a few that were not his by blood. Claiming them was preferable to exposing our failings."

Failings? Did she mean their failing to remain celibate?

"Those of us not chosen to share his bed, well, some of us wanted children. So…"

"Did he know?"

"In some cases, and suspected in others. But he never admitted it."

Rylee spoke now. "Because to do that would be to admit he did not have complete control of his congregation."

Della turned to her and nodded. "I always thought so."

"He's not my father," said Axel, the words spoken aloud as if to convince himself of what he was still afraid to believe.

"Yes, son."

"You are certain?"

"I never slept with the man and I am your mother. So, yes, I'm sure."

Axel released Della and stumbled back, colliding with a wooden bench. He placed a hand on the seat as he fell and thus managed to avoid hitting the ground. The bench shuddered with the force of his landing.

He stared up at his mother as the icy pain in his heart melted away like frost on a spring thaw.

"Who is he, then?"

Her smile faltered. "Do you remember Jack Pritcher?"

Other than Kurt Rogers, Jack Pritcher had been as close to a father as a man could be. In Axel's mind, the big man came back to life. The father figure merging into a father.

"Jack died when I was ten," he said to Rylee.

"He was our carpenter," Della told Rylee and patted the bench as if this were one of Pritcher's creations. "Came from Schenectady. Wife had died, he was older than I was, but he had a kind heart."

A weak heart, Axel remembered, because it was his heart that failed him.

"He came up here after his wife and child died in a terrible car accident. He was a lost soul. I'm sure he never intended to be a father again, but then you came along."

"He never told me," said Axel.

"Not in words. But in other ways. And you have his build. Very trim and muscular. His hair was quite red as a young man, so he told me. And your beard has red highlights."

Axel rubbed the stubble on his cheek.

"Did you two ever think of leaving?"

"Why, no. I loved my work with the animals. I understand them in a way I never understood people. They are more straightforward and no facial expressions to confuse me. Jack seemed content keeping the buildings in good condition. It gave him a purpose. You know what he did back there in Schenectady?"

Axel shook his head.

"He was a fireman. A protector, just like you."

That made his heart ache all over again.

"Della?" asked Rylee. "Why did you tell me where to find the suspect?"

"Suspect?" Her placid expression changed to one of confusion. "I didn't."

"You told us about the wharf," Rylee said, reminding her.

"Yes." Her peaceful smile returned.

"Why?"

Della gave a chuckle as if the question were silly. "Well, because your friend asked me, child. 'Are there any other buildings on the compound?' Those were her exact words. I merely answered her question."

"Because she asked you?" asked Rylee.

Della nodded, seemingly pleased that Rylee now understood.

"What will you do now, Della?" he asked.

"Well, that's a good question. I'm not sure if my older brother is still with us. Perhaps I'll start there. He used to live in Altamont. I remember his address. Also, I've been considering becoming a nun." She swept the veil back up over her hair, wrapping it expertly to cover her head.

Right back into a structured religious community, Axel realized.

"You don't have to, Della. I can take care of you," said Axel.

"Now you sound like my brother. And I don't need taking care of just yet. And though you were always the sweetest boy," she said, "and I'm proud to be your mother, I never really knew how to be one, or a wife. I'm not sure how to explain it, except that I loved Jack, in my way, but I was not in love with him. I don't connect to people in that way. I'm afraid he stayed, hoping I'd change my mind."

Had his father died of a broken heart? Twice broken, he realized. First, at the loss of his wife and child and then, by Della's rejection.

"And he stayed for you, of course." Della beamed at him, her small hands clasped as if in prayer. "He was proud of you. Do you remember carrying his tools? You were his little helper."

Della patted him on the cheek. "I'll write you when I'm settled, shall I?"

"Della, you don't need to join an order," said Rylee. "Our social workers explained that."

"But I will. Perhaps one with animals. That would be nice. I must be somewhere safe for the Rising. Have to be ready." She was now moving back toward the dining hall. Whatever he had expected, it wasn't this. He followed, trailing her back to the entrance. Della paused at the door handle, only because it was metal and she didn't like metal. He remembered that about her, as well.

Rylee opened the door and the trooper within took charge of Della. She never even said goodbye.

The door clicked shut. "I'm sorry, Axel. She's troubled."

He nodded, his teeth tight together and the muscles at his jaw working hard.

"One of our people told me that she's on the spectrum."

It explained everything and nothing. He looked to the empty place where his mother had been. "Yes. I see."

Chapter Twenty-Two

Rylee managed to catch a few hours' sleep and was back at work before nine the next day. They finished up at the compound at noon. Ohr had one final interview with Axel in his office in Kinsley. When Rylee arrived, they were already in the conference room. When she tried to join in, Ohr told her to head back to their offices in Glens Falls.

Rylee just blinked at the order. Instead of moving out, she held the doorknob like it was her last friend and stood momentarily petrified. This was not how she had pictured their goodbye.

"I'll finish up here," said Ohr. "See you back at the office."

Rylee stared at Trace, who stared mutely back, his look expectant.

"All right," she said and closed the door.

Trace's head bowed.

She made it outside, but her footsteps slowed. She wasn't going like this. Instead, she waited outside in the cold for Ohr to emerge. Then she planned to see Axel alone. She had to tell him thank-you, at the very least. And tell him that she loved him? Not that it would change anything; he was staying and she was going.

Kurt Rogers emerged from the coffee shop across the street and ambled over to her.

"They still got him in there?" asked Rogers.

"Yes. Thought we might get a late lunch, but heck. It's closer to dinner now."

Rylee could not keep from fidgeting. She tapped her fingers and sighed. The longer Ohr kept him, the less time she'd have to say goodbye.

"My cat paces like that when she's on the wrong side of the door from her kittens," said Rogers.

Rylee stopped pacing.

"It's the cold."

Rogers leaned against the bench on the sidewalk and glanced at the entrance of the administration building in Kinsley. Dressed in a lambskin coat and wearing gloves, he looked broader and younger. She could see for a moment the stature of the sheriff he must have been.

"What are they doing?" asked Rogers.

"Final interview."

Rogers looked back at the agent in the sedan waiting to drive Ohr back to Glens Falls. Rylee's vehicle was parked just behind that one. In a little while, she'd be in that car, driving away. She should be so happy and proud. Instead, she wanted to scream.

The thought made her heart ache. But what was the choice? He was an elected official here and she'd already been told she was being promoted. New York City, if she wanted, or DC.

Soon, she'd have her choice of postings. It was what she wanted. Wasn't it?

Rogers ambled over to the agent in the vehicle, who lowered the window so they could speak.

Ohr finally emerged from the outer doors, followed by Sheriff Trace.

"You still here?" asked Ohr.

She nodded and turned her attention to Trace, painfully aware of their audience. Her driver had left the vehicle and both she and Rogers watched them. Ohr looked from her to Trace, waiting.

"HELLO, SHERIFF," RYLEE SAID.

His hesitant smile faded. "Agent Hockings," he said, formally. "Thought maybe you left. What can I do for you?"

"I wanted to thank you for rescuing me from the river."

"You already have. And you're welcome."

She couldn't read him. The tension was clear from his expression and the caution in his eyes.

"So, you got what you came here for," he said.

Had she? It seemed something was still missing. Why couldn't she say it to him? She glanced to Rogers and then to Ohr. Finally, she returned her attention to him. Her mouth was so dry.

"Yes, most of it."

"It doesn't all come out like in the movies," he said.

Ohr interjected here. "Our people will be moving to locate and eradicate the manufacturing site. Meanwhile, CDC is creating and stockpiling a vaccine against a possible outbreak. Our diplomatic channels will advocate pursuit of sanctions against North Korea based on evidence that you found."

"You know where they are manufacturing?" asked Axel.

"We have Hal Mondello and Wayne Trace, and both are eager to make a deal. I'm sure our investigation will turn up that information."

She did not mention that they had not succeeded in capturing Hal Mondello's oldest boy, Quinton, thought to have fled to Canada. That bothered Rylee, because he seemed very much in charge of the moonshining operation during her investigation.

Her supervisor turned to Rylee. "Did you tell him you're in line for promotion?"

Rylee's cheeks burned with what felt like shame. It was in part due to Axel's efforts that she'd succeeded. She could not have done any of this without him and the Kowa people. Without them, she'd likely be dead.

Her supervisor continued, "You have done an above average job here, Agent Hockings. Proved me wrong and far exceeded my expectations. You've more than earned that promotion."

Rylee felt none of the pride she had anticipated. She'd spent enough time imagining this moment to know that the twisting dread that tugged at her stomach was not the jubilation she should have been experiencing.

"Congratulations," said Axel, his voice flat and his expression strained.

The time had come to say goodbye. To get on her horse and ride off into the sunset. Specifically, she needed to slip into the faux leather seat of the sedan still sporting the handprints of the Mohawk tribe and point her vehicle south. Instead, she lingered.

Ohr shook Axel's hand and swept away as if in a race-walking competition and finding herself far behind.

Trace watched her go. "Does she always walk like that?"

"Yes, except on inclines."

"Smoking. Steals the wind," he said.

The odor of burning tobacco clung to her clothing and hair the way the tar likely clung to her skin.

He returned his attention to Rylee, moving closer until she could smell the wood smoke that clung to his flannel and the enticing earthy musk of him.

"Where will you go with your promotion? Do you have an office in mind?"

"I was thinking I'd like a bigger posting. New York, of course, or LA, New Orleans because of the port, or Tampa because of the weather."

None of those included the frozen landscape that now surrounded them. And this was only the preview of what winter held in store, when chunks of ice the size of barges would hamper maritime traffic.

"Tampa seems nice," he said with no enthusiasm.

Snowflakes continued to drift down from the blue sky as if confused as to where they had come from and where they belonged. The grass between the sidewalk and curb had become stiff and crunched with each of her shifting steps. But the snow stuck only to the auto-mobiles and the hard cold blacktop of the road surfaces.

Would he ask her to stay? She tilted her chin to look up into his face, blinking at the snowflakes that landed in her eyes.

"No reason to stay here," he said.

She met his stare. "Would you ever leave?"

Had she really said that aloud? The door of possibilities cracked open a bit.

His brows lifted, disappearing into the wool lip of his ski hat.

"I've never lived anywhere else," he said.

"And I've lived everywhere else." She tried for a laugh, failed and cleared her throat. "Funny that trying to get this promotion, and the last one, kept me on the move. When what I said I've wanted was to settle in one place."

"Your job keeps you mobile."

"I might as well be in the army...moving like a migrating bird."

"Maybe the next posting will be a more permanent one."

Rylee felt the tears misting her eyes and choking her throat. Her nose began to run and she wiped it with her leather glove.

"This is all wrong," she said.

"I know. Crazy, right?"

When she imagined a man making a commitment to her, it wasn't in the form of question. As if he were wondering if she could extend her visit for a day or two.

"You can't stay. Can you?" he asked.

He didn't confess his true feelings or express his devotion. His expression looked pained and she wondered if perhaps he'd be happy to see her go and be done with this... Whatever it was they had shared.

They had known each other only a little over a week. It wasn't long enough to fall in love. Was it? This had to be the stress of the case and the danger. Just an encounter.

She scowled. "I should go."

His nod was exaggerated. "Yes, right."

It was looking more and more as if the emotions that were kicking her like a mule were distinctly one-sided.

"Thank you, Sheriff, for all you've done to help me with this case." She extended her gloved hand.

He stared down at it, frowning like a kid who was expecting something specific on Christmas morning and instead got socks.

"Yeah, you're welcome." The handshake was mechanical.

She smiled. "I hope you'll call us if you see anything of which we should be aware."

He held her hand motionless, as if reluctant to let go. Finally, he dropped his hand to his side and then shoved it into his pocket. She could see the balled fist there.

Rylee walked on brittle legs to the driver's side door, gripping the keys as if they were the neck of a snake. She managed to wait until she left the town of Kinsley before the tears began to roll down her cheeks. The sobs came next.

KURT ROGERS CAME to stand beside Axel as the caravan of sedans pulled out like a motorcade.

"You should go after her," said Rogers.

"Nothing for her here, Kurt."

"Just you, I guess." He rested a hand on Axel's shoulder and squeezed. "You tell her you love her?"

He shook his head, knowing that words were just impossible.

"Never took you for a fool, son. Until now, that is."

"Maybe I ought to follow her."

"Sure. Plenty of nice places to go. You two could make a home anywhere." His hand slipped away and he faced the river. "Still, this place is awful pretty, with the snow falling like glitter in the sunlight." He studied the fast-flowing, wide river. "Never get tired of that view. All that water rolling toward the sea and here we sit on this shore, letting it pass by. That's the job, I guess, watching over the folks up here on this side of the river. But you can watch over folks anyplace, Axel. Doesn't need to be here. Follow her and you two can decide where to settle later."

"The town needs me," he said.

"Sure. But what I'm wondering is what *you* need. If it's a woman, all well and good. If it's *that* woman, you best go after her."

Chapter Twenty-Three

Rogers was right again. Axel was letting her get away. He stood in the road, the flurries bringing a dusting of snow. This was his county. He'd been elected to serve as sheriff, and he'd done his job. But he'd stayed to watch over the congregation and stand between the madman at their head and the flock he exploited.

But now they were gone. The women who had raised him had spread out among social services, returning to families or making a lateral move into the arms of another commune. His mother had said her goodbyes and Axel now believed that she had done all she was able to for him. His mother was smart but that part of her that allowed her to connect with people was simply absent. He didn't blame her, but it made him worry. What if he weren't capable of being the kind of parent he had missed? What if he were too damaged by his upbringing?

"What's holding you back, son?" asked Rogers. "Your father is gone. Taken into federal custody, and with all the charges, the only time you'll see him again is on visiting days."

"I won't be visiting. He's not my father."

Rogers lifted his thick white eyebrows. Axel told him the tale.

"You going to change your name? Make it Axel Pritcher?"

"It didn't occur to me."

"Might make a fresh start."

"Maybe. As to Father Wayne, I'll lay odds that he finds his own following in federal prison, but he can't lure vulnerable folks out here. The man was a regular pied piper."

"That's true. But he's gone. That means you can go, too."

Axel turned to look at the old lawman. "You knew that's why I came back?"

"Suspected, is all."

"I still have two years left on my term."

"If you're hanging up your star, I'm not too old to step in until they can do a special election. But try to talk her into coming on back here, if you can."

"Why?"

"Nice place to raise a family. Make me a grandfather, of sorts."

Axel blanched. "I don't even know if she wants a family. And I'm sure I don't know how to be a father."

"The heck you don't. I taught you all you need. Good sense of humor, patience and love. It's not hard, boy. Not as hard as telling the woman you love that you can't live without her. Now that is a job only for the brave at heart."

Axel nodded, glancing back at the empty road.

"Your military record says you are a brave man.

Guess we'll find out if that's so. Get going or you won't catch her until she leaves the county."

THE FLURRIES HAD changed to a light snow that required intermittent wiper blade action. Rylee peered out through the windshield at the precipitation that made visibility difficult. Beyond her windshield, the world looked cold and the road lonely. Time to think about the case and not about Axel. She swallowed the lump of regret, but it stayed wedged like a large cough drop accidentally swallowed.

All the way out of Onutake County, she fought the urge to turn her car around and go back to him. Tell him that she wanted... What? To live at the edge of a northern wasteland? She wanted a home and she wanted Axel. She wanted to stop moving all over the world, but she also wanted a career. How did she make this work? What compromises would she need and which of her objectives would be sacrificed to get the other? It was seldom in life that you reached a point where you could so clearly see two paths.

When she decided not to enlist, she had known it was one such juncture. When she had finished college and joined DHS, she had seen her path and taken charge. But how many of those choices were made not to please herself but to make her father proud?

All of them, she realized. Every one. And if he was proud, he had certainly never told her. Not even when she called him to report that her investigation had led to the arrest of the prime suspect. She could share little else, as the investigation and details were both classified, but his reaction had been typically underwhelming.

"Just part of the job, isn't it?" he had asked her during the brief phone conversation.

Risking her life, getting shot at, diving into a frozen river, just part of the job? It was. But even her supervisors recognized she had gone above and beyond, offered congratulations. They were also putting in for a promotion on her behalf, showing with actions how valuable they considered her service.

The conversation with her father had crystalized that searching for praise from him was pointless. He didn't know how, didn't understand her need for it or just refused to offer even the merest encouragement.

So why was she still acting to please him?

She wasn't. Would not. From this moment she would make choices on what was in *her* best interest.

The wiper blades couldn't keep up with the snow, so she adjusted them again to the next higher setting. The other vehicles from her office had left her behind as they sped along, obviously anxious to be home before dark, while she was in no such hurry.

All she knew for certain was that she had made a huge case, her career was on track and she had never been so miserable.

The misery was the clue to the puzzle. Nothing good should make her feel this sad. Why didn't she see before that leaving Axel would not be like leaving one case for another? He was too important to leave behind. And a week was long enough, obviously, because she was certain that she loved him. But uncertain if he loved her.

At the very least, she should have told him that she had fallen in love with him. The risk of finding out he did not share her feelings now seemed less chilling than not taking the risk and never knowing.

Rylee glanced at the road ahead, the southbound lane of the Northway, searching for an exit or a turn-around that would allow her to change direction. A few miles back, the highway had been a single lane divided only by a yellow line. Now the two directions ran parallel with a median ditch between them.

She considered trying her luck on the snow-covered grass, but the possibility of ending up in the ditch between the divided highway kept her rolling along. Finally, she spotted her chance. The green sign with white letters indicated that the upcoming exit for Exit 26—toward Pottersville and Schroon Lake. Her chance to change direction lay only one mile ahead.

Rylee had been so deep in thought that she had not even noticed that the vehicle behind her was a trooper until the driver hit his lights.

"Really?" she said, glancing from her speedometer to the rearview. "I was only five miles over."

The Northway traffic was light on the two-lane highway, and she easily glided to the shoulder of the exit ramp to Pottersville, followed by the trooper.

It wasn't until the man approached her vehicle that she recognized that he was not in a trooper's uniform and was approaching with his handgun out and raised. She reached for her pistol as she adjusted her view in the side mirror to see the man's face.

Quinton Mondello. Eldest son of Hal Mondello, she realized. The new head of the Mondello family of moonshiners and the one suspected of transporting their North Korean detainee over the US–Canadian border. With no solid evidence of human trafficking, Quinton had been released. He had not been present on the attack at the wharf and had also evaded federal custody at the raid of his family's compound, slipping through the net when they had come to make arrests after the shooting.

He took aim, plainly deciding to shoot her from the back before ever reaching her window. Headlights flashed as a second vehicle pulled in behind Mondello's. His backup, she assumed.

Mondello's first shot missed its mark. Rylee had left her seat and scrambled to the passenger's side as the bullet punctured the rear window and then cleanly through her headrest before shattering the windshield. The fractured windshield was held in place by the protective film but was now a mosaic of tiny cubes of glass.

Rylee exited her vehicle with her pistol drawn and the safety switched off. She used the open door as a shield. Mondello had reached her rear bumper. He had no cover.

She aimed at center mass, making a guess on his position because the light made it impossible to see him clearly.

Her shot broke the side window, showing her that he'd moved. Where was he?

She listened and heard only a vehicle's chime, indicating a door was open. His backup, she realized.

No time to call it in. She needed to move. Rylee reached the front of her vehicle, the engine block providing cover.

"Drop it, Quinton." She recognized the familiar male voice.

"She ruined my family. My father is in jail because of her," said Mondello.

"Your father is in jail for human trafficking that North Korean across the border, and for manslaughter for kicking her into the canal. Did you know what she carried could have killed your whole family?"

Quinton Mondello's voice rose an octave, making him sound crazed. "You're on my list, too, Axel, and you just jumped to the number one spot."

"Drop it or I will shoot you."

Quinton laughed. "You haven't shot at anything or anybody since coming home from the Sandbox. Everyone knows you are scared to shoot. A regular basket case, I hear."

Rylee moved to look around the fender. The two men faced off like gunfighters at high noon. Only Axel's pistol was aimed at Mondello and Mondello's was still pointed in her direction.

Mondello spotted her now and smiled. Their eyes met. He had her now in his sights, and the fact that Axel would kill him after he made his shot seemed to make no difference. Mondello lifted his pistol and two shots fired.

She registered the surprised expression as she put a bullet in his chest. The second one, the one that removed the smug expression along with part of his face, had come from Axel's weapon.

Mondello dropped, inert and lifeless, to the pavement with a sickening whack. Rylee flinched.

Axel ran forward, gun still aimed at Mondello. He reached the still body and placed his foot over the pistol that lay just beyond his curled hand. He stowed the gun in the pocket of his jacket. He made a quick check of Mondello. The sight of his ruined face told Rylee that no one could have survived such a grievous head injury.

Only then did Axel holster his personal weapon and run toward her. She stood to meet him, with time only to slip her gun back into the nylon case.

Then he had her in a crushing embrace. His kisses, frantic, began at her forehead and moved down to her cheek and then to her neck. There he tucked his face into her nape and muttered disjointed words.

"Almost too late… Could have… Almost… My God, Rylee."

"I'm here." She drew back to look at him.

In all the days and all the times they had been together, she had never seen him so pale. He was trembling.

"My hand was shaking. I didn't know if I could make that shot."

And then she remembered that this peace officer had never drawn his pistol since coming home from serving. He had told her he didn't think he could take another life, not even to save his own. Yet, he had done it, to save hers.

"It was my bullet," she said. Trying to take the blame. But they both knew that the way Quintin had dropped, as if his head were no longer connected to his body, meant that it had been Axel's headshot that had killed him.

Her shot had been deadly but not incapacitating. Mondello would have had time to take that shot at Rylee.

Axel seemed to come back into possession of himself. He still looked pale as moonlight, but his gaze was steady as he cradled her head between his two strong hands.

"No. It was mine."

"You saved my life," she said.

"Thank God." He dragged her in for another hug. "Thank God," he whispered into her hair.

"How did you know?"

She drew back, needing answers and to call this in.

Axel blinked at her.

"How did you know Quinton Mondello was following me or that he planned to kill me?"

"I didn't."

She wrinkled her brow, trying to make sense of this.

"Then how did you get here? Why are you here, Axel?"

He let her go and glanced down at the dead body oozing blood onto the road. The thick red fluid oozed along the cracks in the tired pavement.

"Not a good time. Wrong place. Really wrong."

He was muttering again.

"Axel. Look at me."

He did. The trembling had ceased but he looked miserable.

"Why are you here?"

Axel looked at the pavement and the body again. He grasped her hand and pulled her away from the corpse of Quinton Mondello.

"Axel, I have to call this in."

He raked a hand through his hair. "Yes. Call it in. I'll use my radio."

Rylee watched him go. He remained in his vehicle

for a long while after lowering the radio. Finally, Rylee headed back to him.

"Climb in," he said. "It's cold outside. Troopers are en route. Be here in ten."

She climbed into the quiet cab and the two waited in silence. Discussing the events would only taint their statements.

"Thank you for coming for me."

Axel nodded but said nothing.

The sound of sirens was almost immediate.

"How is that possible?" she said, spotting the flashing lights of a large vehicle. Her hand went to the handle of her gun.

"There is a voluntary fire company at the southern half of the exit."

And sure enough, the EMS vehicle rolled down the northbound ramp and across a utility road she had not seen beneath the snow cover. Clearly, this was a well-traveled route by the volunteers.

Soon the quiet stretch of road became an active crime scene and Rylee felt grateful that it was not her corpse being tucked in a body bag and rolled into the back of the emergency vehicle.

AXEL OPTED TO spend the night in a hotel, rather than drive back home. He didn't sleep well and woke with that dull throbbing headache that came from too much caffeine and too little sleep.

He made it to the troopers' station, reviewed and signed his statement. That left one piece of unfinished business and the reason he'd come in the first place: to speak to Rylee.

A text message, a reply and a location chosen, he headed to the small pub and bistro in Schroon Lake. Inside, he was nestled in the aroma of bacon and frying foods. The interior was all knotty pine bedecked with snowshoes and skis from another century. Hand-hewn beams stretched above him, and a kayak hung from between the ceiling fans. Rustic wooden furniture sat before a blazing fireplace and several customers occupied high stools at the bar, cradling their drinks. The men's attention flicked from their drinks to the television, before returning to watch the busy woman behind the bar.

"Welcome," she called. "Sit wherever you like."

He scanned the room but did not find Rylee, so he took a place at a circular table near the stone fireplace and beneath a chandelier made of antlers. Out of habit, he took a seat facing the door and the wide windows that showed the parking lot and the road beyond. The light flurry was now making progress in coating the windshields of the cars parked before the bistro.

He had a cup of coffee that had been refilled once before he saw her step from a vehicle. It wasn't the one she'd driven last night. That one was now in evidence, part of an active investigation. His first shooting and his first kill, at least since coming home from Iraq, or as he thought of it, the Sandbox.

Axel didn't recall leaving the table or the room or the restaurant. But there he was in the lot with the snow floating down lazily and his breath visible in the cold air.

She was talking to herself. Then she sighted him and hesitated in her purposeful stride. Her steps became awkward, as she slipped on the icy pavement before she recovered and continued her forward momentum at a slower pace. She seemed in no hurry to reach him and glanced back at her vehicle with a look he thought might be longing.

Was this meeting an obligation for her, a duty to be discharged? The thought cooled him more than the wintery air. His coat was in his hand. He must have grabbed it on the way out. Axel slipped into it and waited.

"Hello, there," she said. "I didn't expect an escort in."

They faced each other, him feeling uncomfortable in his own skin and her waiting. Should he hug her or kiss her cheek?

Instead, he fell in beside her, grasping her elbow and helping her toward the sidewalk. Her boots were gone and instead she wore the sort of shoes that corporate folks wore. She was changing back to the data analyst she had been.

Already leaving him, he realized. He had to stop her. Suddenly, he forgot how to breathe.

"I'm glad you're all right," she said. "I was just rehearsing how to tell you how grateful I am. That's twice in one week you've backed me up."

It was a job he wouldn't mind taking full-time.

"Getting to be a habit."

"Thank you, Axel, for saving my life. Again."

"You're welcome."

They reached the door to the restaurant and he opened it for her. Like many places in the north, this establishment had a double-door system and a small room that was for waiting in the summer and, in the winter, for keeping the warm air from escaping when guests came and went. Here, they paused between the inside and the outside to face each other.

"You all finished here?" she asked.

"For now. Lots of paperwork, you know."

"I imagine so."

"What about you?" he asked.

"I am all packed up."

She glanced past him to the second door, which led inside, catching a glimpse, he knew, of the log and pine interior.

"It looks like a nice place."

It might be the place they would come back to over the years. That special place where he asked her to be his wife. Or, he thought, it might be that place he avoided forever, never to return.

They moved inside and he led the way back to his table and the cold cup of coffee that waited there.

Rylee took her seat beside him at the pine table. She held her smile as she turned her gaze back on him. Her hand snaked out and clasped one of his, her fingers icy. Their palms slipped over one another and he closed his hand. She gave a little squeeze.

"I know you don't draw your weapon. Haven't, I mean."

"Quinton was right. Not since the Sandbox," he added.

"You fired your weapon. Took the necessary shot. Are you going to be all right with that?" she asked.

"I will be, because I had no other option and my actions kept you here on this earth."

"That just makes me doubly grateful."

Gratitude was not the emotion he wished to engender within her heart.

"I wasn't going to let him hurt you, Rylee. I don't want anything to ever hurt you." And if she'd let him, he'd be there for her, to keep her safe and watch her back. Why couldn't he find the words to tell her so?

Her hand slipped away and the heat of their joined flesh melted from his tingling palm.

"When are you heading back to Kinsley?" she asked.

"That depends."

Outside the windows to their right and left, the snow swirled in the gray afternoon.

"I've been wondering something, Axel." She cocked her head, her eyebrows lifting. Did she know how beautiful she was? Just a look was like a dart piercing his heart.

"You said before that you didn't know about Quinton. That he was coming for me."

The jig was up, he realized. Of course, she'd come back around to that question. "That's true."

"Then why were you there?"

"I love you. I followed you yesterday to tell you that. To get on my knees and ask you to marry me."

"You followed…" Her brow wrinkled, and the corners of her mouth dipped.

Panic seized his heart with sharp incisors.

"Rylee, don't go."

"What?"

"I love you. I don't want you to go."

Now it was her turn to stammer and stare. "Y-you… what? Axel, you've only known me a week."

"Nine days."

"It's not very long."

"Engaged, then. Going steady. Dating. Just not going away."

"My job is in Glens Falls. I'll be transferred soon."

"Yes. I know that. And I don't care. Let me come with you."

Her mouth dropped open and she stared.

"That is a very different offer than asking me to stay."

"It is."

"Axel, are you sure?"

"I'll follow you anywhere, Rylee. If you let me."

She shook her head now, as if not able to understand his words.

"What about your job? You're a county sheriff."

He looked north, perhaps seeing the county and the people there.

"Special election. They'll fill the spot." Now he was looking at her again. "Rylee, I went back there after the military, stayed there because of him."

"Father Wayne?"

"I needed to stop him from killing his followers, my mother, all of them. I knew he'd do it. It was part of his personality. The power of life and death, the ultimate test of his control."

Axel pressed his palms flat to the table.

"I don't need to watch him anymore. End of watch. Mission complete." He stared across the table at her. "Do you understand? I'm free. For the first time in my life I can go anywhere I like, do anything I like and be with whomever I choose." He reached out and she took his hand. "I choose you, Rylee."

"But the county. Your home."

"I hate it there. Hate everything about it, especially the memories. Let someone else take the job. Someone who is there for reasons other than duty."

"Is that really how you feel?"

"Yes."

"What about Kurt Rogers?"

"He'll always be a mentor. I'll visit or he'll visit. But I won't stay in that county. No more."

HE'D BEEN THROUGH so much. Raised in a cult and then fostered. Held in the county by fear and obligation. She thanked God for Kurt Rogers, who had helped Axel find his way. Then the military, where he'd nearly lost himself again. Back to his county, a self-appointed guardian, giving himself the impossible job of curbing a madman, a man who, until recently, he'd believed to be his father.

"Rylee? Say something."

She leaned forward, reaching for him until her fingers stroked the red stubble on his cheek.

"I love you, too, Axel. I just didn't know how we could make this work between us. But now I see nothing but possibilities."

"Is that a yes?" he asked.

"Yes to the engagement."

He rose from his seat and pulled her into his arms, kissing her with passion before the great stone fireplace in the middle of a restaurant with few customers to witness their union.

When she drew back, her face was flushed and she beamed up at him.

"What should we do now?" he asked.

"I was hoping to buy you lunch." She smiled and offered her hand.

"Yes. Lunch."

She stood beside him, still holding his hand as she spoke. "And after that, a life together."

Together, they would make the permanent home that she had always wanted and raise the family for which he had always longed. They were together at last and forever, just as they were always meant to be.

* * * * *

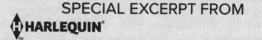
"Why did you say you owed me?" she asked.

The question came out of the blue and threw him, so much so that he gulped down too much coffee and nearly choked. Hardly the reaction for a tough-nosed cop. But his reaction to her hadn't exactly been all badge, either.

Kellan lifted his shoulder and wanted to kick himself for ever bringing it up in the first place. Bad timing, he thought, and wondered if there would ever be a good time for him to grovel.

"I didn't stop Eric from shooting you that night." He said that fast. Not a drop of sugarcoating. "You, my father and Dusty. I'm sorry for that."

Her silence and the shimmering look in her eyes made him stupid, and that was the only excuse he could come up with for why he kept talking.

"It's easier for me to toss some of the blame at you for not ID'ing a killer sooner," he added. And he still did blame her, in part, for that. "But it was my job to stop him before he killed two people and injured another while he was right under my nose."

The silence just kept on going. So much so that Kellan turned, ready to go back to his desk so that he wouldn't continue to prattle on. Gemma stopped him by putting her hand on his arm. It was like a trigger that sent his gaze searching for hers. Wasn't hard to find when she stood and met him eye to eye.

"It was easier for me to toss some of the blame at you, too." She made another of those sighs. "But there was no stopping Eric that night. The stopping should have happened prior to that. I should have seen the signs." When he started to speak, Gemma lifted her hand to silence him. "And please don't tell me that it's all right, that I'm not at fault. I don't think I could take that right now."

Unfortunately, Kellan understood just what she meant. They were both still hurting, and a mutual sympathyfest was only going to make it harder. They couldn't go back. Couldn't undo. And that left them with only one direction. Looking ahead and putting this son of a bitch in a hole where he belonged.

Don't miss Safety Breach *by Delores Fossen,*
available December 2019 wherever
Harlequin® Intrigue books and ebooks are sold.

Harlequin.com

Need an adrenaline rush from nail-biting tales
(and irresistible males)?

Check out **Harlequin Intrigue®**,
Harlequin® Romantic Suspense and
Love Inspired® Suspense books!

New books available every month!

CONNECT WITH US AT:

Facebook.com/groups/HarlequinConnection

 Facebook.com/HarlequinBooks

 Twitter.com/HarlequinBooks

 Instagram.com/HarlequinBooks

 Pinterest.com/HarlequinBooks

ReaderService.com

H HARLEQUIN®
™

**ROMANCE WHEN
YOU NEED IT**

SGENRE2018R

Love Harlequin romance?

DISCOVER.

Be the first to find out about promotions, news and exclusive content!

Facebook.com/HarlequinBooks

Twitter.com/HarlequinBooks

Instagram.com/HarlequinBooks

Pinterest.com/HarlequinBooks

ReaderService.com

EXPLORE.

Sign up for the Harlequin e-newsletter and download a free book from any series at **TryHarlequin.com.**

CONNECT.

Join our Harlequin community to share your thoughts and connect with other romance readers!
Facebook.com/groups/HarlequinConnection

**ROMANCE WHEN
YOU NEED IT**

HSOCIAL2018